THE BRUMBACK LIBRARY

OF VAN WERT CO

VAN WERT, C

Death in Equality

Death
in
Equality

Lucinda Ebersole

ST. MARTIN'S PRESS
NEW YORK

F
EBE

Design by Nancy Resnick

Library of Congress Cataloging-in-Publication Data

Ebersole, Lucinda.
    Death in Equality / by Lucinda Ebersole. — 1st ed.
        p.   cm.
    ISBN 0-312-15106-3
    I. Title.
PS3555.B483D4   1997
813'.54—dc20   96-36724
                                                    CIP

First Edition: March 1997

10   9   8   7   6   5   4   3   2   1

*For
Edwina Payne,
who took me to the endless realm of poetry*

Acknowledgments

To Sir Stephen Spender, because sometimes poetry is enough.

To all those people who have read this manuscript in various stages: Nancy Alvarez, Diane Apostolos-Cappadona, Amy Bloom, Jane Bradley, Shirley Graves Cochrane, Christin Everly, Patricia Browning Griffith, Richard Peabody, Beverly Cleghorn Ricks, and Sandra Walker.

To Harry Lowe for the Farm.

To Terri Merz and Robin Diener and the people at Chapters Bookstore.

To Connie Imboden for her photography, especially this cover.

To Ann Burrola for her friendship.

To Michael Denneny for his help and encouragement.

And to my editor, Keith Kahla.

Death
in
Equality

*T*here is nothing but death in Equality. It has been that way for some time. What does one do these days in Alabama? Raise cotton? Cane? Play football? Equality was bypassed by industry, by agriculture, and even by the highway that runs between Birmingham and Montgomery. Death is the only industry in Equality. Death has brought me here. Death and memory.

Once upon a time, Equality had a lumber mill and a cotton mill, but they are gone now. The lumber is easier to chip into pulp. Giant machines with great steel arms reach out and hug the trees, pulling them close as they are sheared by spinning blades. The machines dump them once they are dead. Dump them into chippers that chew and spit the trees directly onto barges that take them away to foreign ports.

Cotton is no longer king. The white balls hold memories too painful to remember. With no cotton there is no mill. No labor in Equality, only death. Death and memory.

The memories brought me back.

The memories and the fact that there is nowhere else to go.

This is the end.

I will end where I should have begun.

It will end with a memory.

I remember the sounds of the pine logs being shaped into sheet after sheet of lumber.

I remember the cars filling the roads at the beginning and end of the second shift at the cotton mill.

I remember women whose hands were scarred from picking the white balls of cotton from the spiny husks.

I remember the red clay.

I remember history.

Most days I can no longer remember what day it is. I have no family left. I am the end of the line. The last Cordelia. The seventh Cordelia. Unlucky seven. Seven generations of Cordelias born or died in Equality. I was not born here, but why buck tradition. I will die here. It will come soon. All I have is a history. A past. No future. This is what has brought me to Equality. Death.

For the remaining time that I will live, I live in the house my great-great-grandfather built. There was nothing then. Nothing in Equality but a general store and a train station and a handful of farms. Now the house sits surrounded by doctors' offices and McDonald's. There are now three funeral homes in Equality, but once there was just this house. For me, there is just this house. The seventh and last Cordelia alone in the house with thoughts and memories. I am having fewer and fewer thoughts, only memories. Most of the memories are of death in Equality, death and poetry, bits and pieces of words and phrases. Words were my life, but now the words escape me. There are fragments of the words of other people, but where are my stories?

Several of my stories have seen the printed page. But I will never hold my book in my hands as I held so many other people's books. I have edited them and celebrated when they sat on a shelf in a bookstore. I will never celebrate for my own book. The stories die with me. Harper Lee wrote that people bring food with death and flowers with illness and little things in between. The nurse-practitioner brings flowers sometimes when she visits. Flowers from her yard on Hickory Street, the street by the Methodist church. Sometimes, the old people from the church stop by to see me, the people who remember the fifth Cordelia and the sixth.

The man who delivers Meals on Wheels delivered them to the fifth Cordelia, my grandmother. She died five years ago, two weeks after her one hundredth birthday. It had been just we two; now there is just me. Mr. Delaney, the man who brings the food, is eighty-six, twice my age. He says to me, "You should be bringing this food to me. It's a shame." I want to tell Mr. Delaney he is wrong. There is no shame in dying. Everyone does it at some time or another; still, they seem loath to accept it.

Doctor Campbell comes by each week and always says it should be him dying, not me. His practice is gone now. Gone to a grandson. The fourth-generation doctor in the Campbell family. Three of them in Equality. Doctor Campbell's son escaped the family history and took a lucrative offer from the University of Alabama at Birmingham, the famous UAB complex. He wanted his son to teach with him, but when his son finished his residency, he came back to Equality and worked with his grandfather. The youngest Doctor Campbell will probably be the last Doctor Campbell in Equality. There are few young families living here now. There is not much chance of supporting a family here anymore, unless you're a doctor.

The youngest Doctor Campbell is my age. The last Doctor Campbell takes care of the last Cordelia. He, like me, has the memories. Red clay stains his hands, and so he returned to care for the elderly, the infirm, and a lone writer whom his grandfather says is dying before her time. For everything there is a season and a time for every matter under heaven. Ecclesiastes. A time for everything under heaven.

Who decides the time to die? Not the doctor who would go in my place. He is no longer a happy man now that he can no longer see patients, so he has adopted me. I am his fantasy. There is nothing he can do for me; he cannot kill me, he cannot prescribe medicine, he cannot save me. So he visits me and pretends. Mostly, he talks about the dead.

It's so unusual, he tells me. Now, your mother, that was expected, even she was rather young—sixty-four. The youngest dead Cordelia, save for me. The rest of the Cordelias lived past their ninetieth birthdays—long, prosperous lives—bore children, nursed others, lived long and prospered. I have no children. I have no book. There is no other Cordelia to nurse me. All I have is the truth.

Doctor Campbell says he will tell me the truth. He has seen the reports from the lab. Lace. Lace, he says. Your lungs are like lace. My mother's lungs were like lace. Doctor Campbell had said the same thing to me when she was sixty-four and dying. So delicate an image. My lungs like a fine tatted lace. My mother's condition was expected. She had smoked since she was fourteen. I have never smoked and neither has Doctor Campbell—two non-smokers dying of lung cancer. He says it is a joke, a joke from God. I don't think God is such a joker.

It is not like I didn't want to smoke. I had always wanted to. Perhaps it was from years of watching my mother smoke. My mother, Bette Davis, Lauren Bacall—I would join them. I would smoke small dangerous cigarettes—Gauloises or Gitanes. I would wear a white T-shirt and roll the pack in the sleeve. I would be a rebel. But every time I lit a cigarette, I got sick. I even got sick if I spent too much time in a room with my mother's smoke. Still, it was an ambition of mine.

When I was twelve, I saw some pictures in a *Photoplay* of Lee Radziwill and Rudolph Nureyev. They were kissing. Each frame caught a different section of the kiss. I still have the pictures. They are in an envelope filled with pictures of Lee Radziwill.

She was my idol as a child.

She did what she wanted.

She kissed Rudolph Nureyev.

She smoked.

In my favorite picture of her, she is half sitting—propped—against a table wearing a real short skirt. She has a cigarette in one hand and a drink in the other. When she saw the picture she was said to have remarked that when one reaches a certain age, one should be more dignified.

At twelve, I was not terribly dignified. I announced to Mother my ambition in life—to drink, to smoke, and to kiss Rudolph

Nureyev. I will never forget my mother's words—grounded for life. My mother has won. At forty-three I am grounded for life. I never kissed Rudolph Nureyev. I never smoked. Now I am dying and there is no one to buy me liquor. It will interfere with the medicine, the doctor tells me. He is the same doctor who tells me that I haven't much time. The doctor whose grandfather tells me my lungs are like lace—who tells me God is a joker.

Death is Doctor Campbell's joke. He has made a game of death and I am the other player. He has a contest going to see who will die first. He is a gambler—a boy in an old man's body, and he likes the idea of sport. Every day he sees me it is sport— he plays this game alone. He wants to outlive me. I am no competition for the old man. I do not care when it happens. There is no one left to say good-bye.

If I were a gambler, I would bet on the aged doctor.

If I were a gambler, I would write this story—write about death as I wrote about life.

I write.

I am a writer.

I was a writer.

I am the greatest unpublished writer of my generation.

Now I think about being a writer.

It hurts more than the cancer—the novels in the drawer.

Perhaps I really didn't want it enough.

Perhaps I wasn't good enough.

Perhaps the timing was wrong.

And now the time is gone.

Cordelia was never fond of first person. She always liked to have an omniscient narrator handy to tell her stories. Her stories had a voice that could look into the heart and souls of her characters and tell the world what they were thinking, a kind of intellectual eavesdropping, she would say. One would never have thought that one day she would need a narrator of her own, but that's fate for you. Some days, she is just too weak to tell her own stories, and now there is only time to tell the stories. She has waited too long to get them into print. Oh, one or two have been published and she enjoyed it, but she remains the steadfast writer who will always tell you that she is writing for herself and for no one else, so publish or not, it really doesn't matter. This is the writer's "high road," the artistic path to literary fulfillment. Actually, dying might be just the boost Cordelia's career needs. It did wonders for Sylvia Plath. Breece D'J Pancake didn't have a book published until he shot himself. John Kennedy Toole was hailed a genius after twenty years of his mother's insistence that it was so. Of course, this could be a problem for Cordy, since her mother is already dead and would never have thought her a genius.

Writers come and go. They have the shelf life of your average literary magazine. Some writers publish to big advances and summer on the Cape. They publish in the *Paris Review,* a rare example of a literary magazine that has endured, though some would say its endurance is in large part due to its endowment. Cordelia struggled along like so many, editing, proofreading, a grant here and there. She has outlived many literary magazines, *Vagabond, Sun & Moon, The Outsider, Noble Savage, American Review, Gargoyle, Antaeus,* and many others that she never read. When she first heard the dreaded "C" word, she thought of all the books she hadn't read. There was a stack of new novels by the bed, a history of opera, Kristeva on Proust, the volumes of poetry she had meant to get to, the volume of Virginia Woolf's letters that she lacked, the out-of-print volumes that she would never find, the first novel to complete the collection of an author, *War and Peace, One Hundred Years of Solitude, Gravity's Rainbow, Flaubert's Parrot,* she had meant to read them. She went home from the doctor's office. He said to get a second opinion, but she sat in her apartment and read. Now she can no longer read. It's too much effort to hold the book, to focus her eyes, to comprehend the words. She has spent an entire life in a world of words, and now she fights to remember simple phrases, a line from a poem she once quoted in its entirety, the title of a book, the last, great lines . . . and so we beat on, boats against the current, borne back ceaselessly to the past; someone threw a dead dog after him down the ravine; I am thinking of aurochs and angels, the secret of durable pigment, prophet sonnets, the refuge of art. And this is the only immortality you and I may share, my Lolita; his eyes were empty and blue and serene again as cornice and facade flowed smoothly once more from left to right, post and tree, window and doorway and signboard, each in its ordered place; you are ravishing; the grace of the Lord Jesus Christ be with you all. Amen.

Some days are better than others.

Some days, I find myself floating.

Some days, I think it is the end.

Some days, I wake up again.

I was taught as a child that "I" was the least important word in the dictionary. That is why I never write in the first person. I prefer the third person. I like omniscient narrators. I like God.

Today the nurse comes to give me injections. She is one of the few, like the youngest Doctor Campbell, to be young and have a family. She is a gambler like the old doctor. She is gambling that I will survive to see her child born. I am not a gambler. Gabrielle Fletcher is her name, and she, like so many of us, is in Equality because of the memory. Minnie Bruce Pratt says it's a smell of red dirt under the nails. Gabrielle's great-grandfather came to Equality from New Orleans from France. A mechanical man, yet illiterate. His grandson, Gabrielle's uncle, died in World War II. It is a story of legend.

I ask her about it. The story I wrote was different but the same. Gabrielle does not want to talk about the past. Her own mother was just a baby when it happened. It has been blown out of proportion, she says. When she visits she gives me injections. I have always hated needles. My veins are small and I can feel the needle rubbing the insides of my veins. I bruise easily. More so since the cancer. Gabrielle works hard to find veins. The injection will slow the pain, but it is painful to end the pain.

I wonder which is worse—the pain, which is constant, or the pain to end the pain, which is coupled with dread and anxiety?

Which is worse—to have pain and have thoughts or to end the pain and float in memory?

allons danser . . .

*O*kay, Cordelia. I know you hate this but it will help with the pain."

"Help me have more pain?"

"Answer this question while I find a vein. What is the capital of Italy?"

"Rome."

"What is the capital of Bosnia?"

"Chechnya."

"No. Chechnya is a new republic in the Soviet Union."

"Moscow."

"Good. I think I've found one. What's the capital of Algeria?"

"Marrakech."

"Algiers. That was an easy one."

"Do you know Amy Hempel?"

"Is she from around here?"

"She's a writer. She wrote a story called 'In the Cemetery Where Al Jolson Is Buried.' There's a woman dying in the story. She asks the narrator to tell her only the things she won't need to remember. Like the difference between Bosnia and Chechnya. This stuff makes me float. I feel like I'm suspended under water. Drowning while living. Floating yet drowning. It makes me stupid."

"But you don't have much pain."

"I think I would rather die painfully than stupid. I hate first person."

"What?"

"Bosnia."

To look down on her, you would never know she was sick. Well, maybe she is a bit too still. She was always one to toss and turn. In the mornings her bed would look like it had been stripped. She fought her dreams and they fought back. She slept, really slept, only after the sun was up. That is why she was never much of an early riser. But it is a hard thing to convey to other people—fighting dreams. The injections deprive her of dreaming. The dreaming part of her floats up here and looks down on her drunken sleep. It has been a good life, being an omniscient narrator of the stories that she has told. Without the dreams there are only already-told stories. The problem with being an omniscient narrator is that one needs to be inexorably linked to a storyteller—with a person who lives life and lets the narrator watch and tell. But when the storyteller dies, the narrator dies, no matter how omniscient the reader may have thought she was. There are now only old stories.

Christopher's story had always intrigued her. There is a fine line between fact and fiction. The good storyteller takes the facts and makes them better—the way things would have been with the omnipresent eye of the omniscient narrator. Christopher, Gabrielle's uncle, was like too many of the people in Equality. If he were alive, he would still be living here. Like Gabrielle, like the youngest Doctor Campbell, like Cordelia, he was a boy cursed with memory. Like Cordelia, he was a dream fighter. Unlike Cordelia, his dreams won.

Christopher strained to hear the voices, listened for some recognition, but in the end all he could hear was the scrape of the rope across the branch and the boy's voice trailing off, "Don't . . . please, please." The sound of the voice always woke Christopher from the dream. The cold, muddy trench on the scarred soil of Germany was a far cry from the warm banks of Hatchet Creek, and as Christopher fingered the Luger, he realized just how far he was from Equality, Alabama.

"Calm down, son," the sergeant said as he steadied Christopher's shoulder. "We'll be moving out soon. Try to rest."

The sun was beginning to rise as Christopher tugged on his jacket sleeve, rubbing the khaki over the barrel of the Luger. He thought he could still see the small, almost feminine fingerprints of the dead soldier's hand as he looked at the gun. Unable to get the dream out of his mind, he continued to polish the souvenir and remember the hanging.

Christopher had often seen the colored boy in town, and though he had been unable to recall his name, he knew the boy had finished school and was a good worker. His grandfather had said so—"That one's a good worker"—and he would know. He had landed in Mobile on a French freighter when he was fourteen and never went back. There wasn't a piece of machinery that he couldn't fix, but he could never read.

On the day of the night the dream started, the two boys were fishing on different parts of the bank. The colored boy sat on a rock catching one fish after another. He was a good worker even when he was fishing, Christopher thought, as he looked at his own empty stringer. Hearing the sudden rustling of leaves behind him, Christopher turned to see the long black body from the rock, arm outstretched, offering a rusted snuff can half full of night crawlers. Christopher took the can, relishing the live bait. Then he was sorry that he had not asked the boy his name. Now he is glad he didn't.

Snapping turtles took the worms as quickly as they hit the water. Christopher gathered his belongings and climbed the bank toward the pecan tree. The stillness of the creek bed was broken by voices.

"Don't, please," a voice pleaded. Other voices were distant and muffled. Christopher moved close enough to hear the rope hit a branch.

"Tie his hands."

"Please, no."

He saw the noose dangling and, as he inched forward, he saw the face of his fishing companion. Christopher opened his mouth but could only watch. The boy stood on a five-gallon bucket that was kicked away. It should have been the end, but the long black body stretched, allowing the tips of his toes to rest on the ground.

"Damn."

Again, he stood on the bucket as one of the men dug a hole. He only dug a few inches. Christopher prayed that something would happen, that the boy would break free, that the hole would be too shallow, but the hanging continued. As the boy was pushed from the bucket to the grave, Christopher saw his eyes.

Everyone in Equality talked about the hanging. The hole beneath the pecan branch remained. Some dismissed its constant excavation as a childish prank, but many believed the ghost of the colored boy returned each night, sweeping away the dirt as a constant reminder of what happened. Christopher never talked about the hanging, but he saw the ghost often in his dreams. Many times he sat on the rock on the bank of Hatchet Creek hoping the ghost would appear, arm outstretched, and offer him absolution.

A year after the hanging, Christopher's grandfather died and a year after that, Christopher left Equality and joined the army.

As a young boy, Christopher had read of Europe and listened as his grandfather told tales of France—*Olympia* in the Jeu de Paume in Paris, the Cathedral at Chartres, the *Isenheim Altarpiece* at Colmar. He was still a boy, but the Europe he marched across was not the one in the stories. Clouds floated above his head in the sunshine and he knew that same sun shone on Equality. His thoughts drifted like the clouds, only to be brought back to reality by the voice of his sergeant.

"Stop the goddamn daydreaming," he shouted. "This war ain't over until you boys are home. You can relax then. Now, you better damn well stay alert."

"Hey, Chris, I bet we'll be home next month," said the boy from Kansas who'd just joined the unit.

Christopher was taken aback. He'd never been "Chris." The informality in the salutation so occupied his mind that he didn't respond. He was glad that his grandfather had not lived to see Paris fall.

"Do you really think they're killing all those people?" the gangly redhead asked.

"That's why we're here, Red," said the boy from Kansas with a naive enthusiasm. "Killing the enemy is what it's all about."

All the soldiers had heard the rumors. Death was the favorite topic of conversation.

"Compound," called the scout. "It's about a hundred yards. Looks deserted."

The company fell to the ground, crawling cautiously forward. Christopher felt the wind blow over his body while a sprig of edelweiss swayed and the sun warmed his back. He strained his neck and looked at the sky. An acrid smoke now mingled with the clouds. The sergeant yelled, "Move out," and the company scrambled to their feet and burst forth, guns drawn, into the camp.

Bodies hung from gallows: The air hung with silence. The camp appeared to be deserted, but the sergeant knew to trust nothing. Approaching a series of wooden sheds, he broke down a flimsy door expecting to confront the enemy. The room was dank and bare, furnished with rows of large shelves. At first he thought he'd found a morgue, for the shelves held emaciated bodies. Then the sergeant stepped back as some of the bodies moved toward him.

Walking out into the breeze, the sergeant regrouped. They needed to be together to get through this. He felt like a teacher trying to preserve order on the day before Christmas break.

Shouting orders, he tried putting names with faces when he realized that the company had scattered. One was missing.

Christopher viewed the bodies hanging from the gallows. In his mind each face was the same; all eyes focused on him. Looking at the gallows, he saw the pecan tree at Hatchet Creek. He saw the colored boy's ghost as he looked at the darkened faces of the corpses, their tongues protruding.

In the distance he saw a stack of firewood like his grandfather used to cut. Remembering the smell of fresh wood and the symmetry of the pile wedged between two small trees—shoulder high in September, knee high in April—he longed for Equality and the familiar smells of home. But the memories had deceived him.

Before him lay a hundred decaying bodies, stacked as he used to stack his grandfather's wood. He dropped his rifle, horror subsiding as the death around him became as natural as the decay in a compost.

Christopher moved from the cord of corpses toward a row of furnaces like the one in the high school basement that his grandfather repaired every school year. He dragged his fingers across the doors, some warm, some still hot, burning the tips of his fingers. He grabbed the handle of the last furnace, opening it to allow in the sunshine. Among the ashes were the bodies of children. Christopher saw their frightened eyes as he climbed in, his heavy army boots cracking bones like pecan shells on an autumn day. The door swung closed after him and he sat with his back to the warm wall and cradled one of the children. Christopher opened his mouth, his voice echoed.

> *"Jesus loves the little children*
> *All the little children of the world."*

The metal chamber transformed his single voice into a choir.

A fine ash filtered down from the sky like snow, making it easy to follow Christopher's footprints. The sergeant found the rifle on the ground and headed for the ovens. He could hear the muffled singing as he drew closer and opened the last door. Christopher was blinded by the bright light flooding in. Clutching the child tightly to his body, he grabbed for the Luger, firing wildly.

The sergeant took cover beside the furnace, drawing his gun. The single bullet sounded like a bell in a distant church tower. He listened, knowing he would hear no sounds, and, lowering his gun, turned back and stood before the furnace. Gently, he closed the door, as the silence was broken by the sounds of reinforcements rolling into the camp.

I knew the story would wake her. Cordelia read that thoughts keep you from sleeping. A blank mind is a mind that can fall asleep at will. The great thinkers of our time were said to have required little sleep. Martha Graham never slept more than three hours a night. Cordelia was never much of a sleeper. She was up and down all through the night, writing down dreams, taking notes, turning the computer off and on.

Her eyes were beginning to move. I don't like watching her lie so still. Her restlessness has always kept me alert, waiting to take over the narration of any story she might tell. She has given up on telling the stories, but she still remembers them. The stories she wants to remember are the stories of death. They are the stories that offer her comfort as she faces her own death. What are the telltale signs of death? Floating above her, I find the stillness is unbearable. When the end does come, will I crash to the ground? There is a fear of falling. Her life is the only thing that allows me to float in the void, breathing air like water. It is her life that lets me see into the minds of all the characters and tell you what they are thinking without their knowing. I can see into their own hearts when they themselves cannot. I believe that Cordelia is one of those rare individuals who can turn the fear of falling into an art.

Her eyes roll around like the giant marble that works the

mouse in her PowerBook. Cordelia was not content with the uniform gray ball of the computer. Life is filled with infinite grays, but not the mouse ball. One afternoon Cordelia went into the Red Balloon, her favorite children's toy store. Cordelia never went into the store that she didn't leave with a bag filled with toys. Her justifications for acquiring many of the items were far more entertaining than the items themselves.

The Fortune Telling Fish was only fifty cents, much cheaper than the psychic network. The phone psychic charged $3.95 a minute but the Fortune Telling Fish would always be at hand. In fact, that was the way it worked. One lays the fish in the palm of the hand and asks questions. The curl of the body provides the answer, all in the palm of your hand.

The marble wasn't easy. She needed to make the PowerBook more colorful. It needed a personality. She spent nearly an hour looking at marbles. A personality is not a quick purchase. She cradled each potential personality in her hand, feeling the texture of the glass on her fingertips. She held them to the light and watched the colors refract. Her final choice was blue, with a bright swatch of yellow on one side. At the pinpoint of color where the yellow ended, it fused with the blue, fanning out into a calm, earthy green. Cordelia said the blue was traditional and dependable; yet it was infused with the insanity of the bright yellow. Together at a point they mingled for a calming patch of green. It reflected Cordelia's personality, steady and traditional with a wild, insane streak. It was the yellow of her personality that made her write. It was the yellow that sent her into the Red Balloon.

The marble was not an exact fit, but sat slightly removed from its surroundings, as though it didn't want the gray of the computer to fade onto its shiny colors. The marble sits in its computer socket like Cordelia's eyes sit in their sockets. They no longer fit exactly, like they are trying to keep death from fading into them. Her eyes are the only things that move in her bed, her eyes and her fingers that tap the remote control of the stereo changer. She used to fight the bed, but now she is still and quiet. Only the eyes move. They dance beneath her eyelids. In that brief second between sleep and wakefulness, that moment just as her eyes start to open, in the blur of darkness and light, she sees me floating above her. In the consciousness of light, she never sees me, but she knows that I am here, watching and telling.

Once I had free rein to go and come as I pleased, to follow the wildest adventures of her imagination, to see people and enter their deepest thoughts and feeling, even if they had no thoughts or feeling. On the day she closed the PowerBook, hiding the blue marble, she came to this bed. She used to think that bedrooms were too small and intimate for omniscient narrators, but the cancer changed that notion. On the day she closed the computer on the blue and yellow marble, she found the Fortune Telling Fish in the drawer. She held it in her hand, but the fish didn't move.

I knew the story would wake her.

*A*uschwitz was an awful place to die. It was a place to fight to live. It was a place of yellow stars, not yellow suicides. He made a mistake. Christopher hadn't meant to kill himself. He panicked. Think about where he was. Who he was. He just panicked.

Primo Levi was liberated from Auschwitz in 1945.

Primo Levi committed suicide in 1987.

Tadeusz Borowski survived the gas of Auschwitz and Dachau.

Tadeusz Borowski gassed himself in 1951.

Paul Celan hauled rocks in Romania.

Paul Celan died by his own hand, didn't die the mauve death.

> *I pilot you behind the world,*
> *there you are with yourself, unflinching,*
> *serene*
> *the starlings take a survey of death,*
> *the reeds sign a warning to stone, you have*

everything
for this evening.

The capital of Romania is Bucharest.

I have never been to Bucharest. I have never set a single story in Bucharest.

I write about Equality.

So does Jane.

Jane.

I have Jane's first collection of stories. Not many people read them but I read every word. The book was like a manual for me because I wanted to get out of Equality and be a writer and Jane was the only person to have ever accomplished such a feat. It was quite a feat for Jane. Once, in New York City, I went to hear her read. Her voice had a slight hint of Equality. The memories covered her face like red clay. I have never seen anyone with the memories so close to the surface. She read from the novel, the one that was nominated for a National Book Award. Her voice broke several times as she read, but she never stopped. Jane told the truth. When it was over I told her. I said I was from Equality and I asked her to sign my books, the new novel and the short stories.

Jane held the slim volume of stories.

"You have one of the five copies that ever sold," she said. "Do you go back?"

"For Christmas. Have you been back?"

"Only once."

Jane signed my books and gave me her card. She told me to keep writing. I heard that she had stopped. She no longer puts pencil to paper. She has a cabin in Taos and she no longer writes. I want to know why, but I could never bring myself to ask her. Perhaps it is true that everyone has one story. Jane told her story, wrote a book, and is living happily ever after. I said I only wanted one book and I would live happily ever after. Now I won't even live. Jane came back once. Once to see Cora.

$\mathcal{I}$t's an odd thing. One tiny place creating two talented souls. Truman Capote and Harper Lee lived next door to each other in Monroeville, Alabama. Jean Seberg was a baby-sitter for Mary Beth Hurt. Jean would act out parts and tell the children she was going to be an actress. She would leave Marshalltown, Iowa, and go to Hollywood and become a movie star. Mary Beth said she would go, too. Jane and Cordelia grew up on opposite sides of the tracks in Equality.

Cora died when Cordelia was just a child. She hadn't read Jane's stories, but she was already a storyteller. Cordelia didn't see Jane come back for that one visit. But she knew Cora. Everyone in Equality knew of Cora Johnson. First, there was her imposing figure. She weighed almost 250 pounds. Her weight left her plagued with high blood pressure and diabetes. It was a wonder that she had survived as long as she had. She had raised two sons, each preceding her in death. One died a hero in World War II, and the other died of a heart attack in Detroit. The son in Detroit had been a preacher and was the father of her one grandchild, Dexter. Dexter left his family in Detroit to stay with his grandmother until the end. He was there when Jane came back.

$\mathcal{D}$exter didn't know his grandmother very well. He had been raised in Detroit, and the family seldom came back to the South. He begged Cora to come and live with them in Detroit, but she refused. She had lived in Alabama all her life and in her house for sixty-two years—through two children, three miscarriages, wars, deaths, disasters, and depression, both her country's and her own. She would die in that house.

What Dexter did know of Cora was that she had always been a strong force in the black community, even when it was the colored community. She was one of those people who kept calm in a crisis, who seemed to have the right thing to say at the right time and the ability to keep quiet when the time was wrong for words. She always spoke her mind, and she always did as she pleased.

Dexter remembered thinking of Cora when he looked at his own son. They were kindred spirits even though they had never met. Dexter sometimes worried about the absence of contact between the two. Why had he never brought his son to meet Cora? It had not been an intentional omission, but there was work and school and other excuses Dexter couldn't name. He should have flown her to Detroit to see his son graduate with honors from Wayne State, but that was last year. Time had caught up with them, and though the grandmother and the son were cast from the same mold, they would never sit side by side. Still, Dexter thought, had they met, Cora and Dexter Junior—or Ahmad, as he now called himself—would have been fast friends.

Friends were something Cora had plenty of. Dexter was amazed at the number and the organization of her friends. Each day, as though someone had set a limit, no more than five people came to see her. Mrs. Walker was the one who came every day. Cora had delivered her when the doctor couldn't come for her mother, and they had worked in the school lunchroom together until Cora retired. One person brought food each day, and one read to her from the Bible. Usually, one or two other people stopped by to say hello, or good-bye. Equality was definitely not Detroit.

On this particular day, Cora's preacher had come to read to her. Mrs. Walker had done double duty and brought in food. She and Dexter stood in the kitchen drinking coffee. They watched out the window as a car pulled into the backyard. It stopped abruptly, stirring up a cloud of red dust that enveloped the new Chevrolet. The dust settled on the white car and seemed to change its color.

The driver of the car sat behind the wheel for some time. Dexter assumed that she was lost and would regain her bearing and drive off. Instead, she got out of the car and walked to the back door. Dexter knew she was lost. She was not a local, he said to Mrs. Walker. He could tell that by the way she was dressed.

The woman wore silk trousers and a matching navy silk jacket. She wore a beige silk shirt that matched the soft kid boots on her feet. Her blond hair framed her face, and her eyes were obscured by large, dark Ray-Ban sunglasses. Dexter knew the brand name because Dexter Junior—Ahmad—had a pair just like them. He went to the door, but knew he could offer little help. As she stood on the other side of the screen, the woman spoke. Dexter noticed the slight tinge of a Southern accent as she asked, "Is Cora home?"

Dexter was flustered. He didn't answer. He attempted to open the screen, but pulled it instead of pushing it. He corrected his mistake and finally allowed the woman to enter at the same time he answered her question.

"Yes," he said. He was going to lead her to his grandmother's bedroom, but she knew the way.

"Hello, Mrs. Walker," she said as she disappeared from the kitchen.

"Who was that?" Dexter asked Mrs. Walker.

"I have no idea. Looked like she was off the television. I have no idea," she said.

They followed the woman to the bedroom. She was sitting on the edge of Cora's bed. Her dark clothing made her body blend in with the deep blue comforter. She held Cora's hand, which was twice as big as her hand and as black as a starless night. The woman's hand was small and pale, almost translucent with her rosy knuckles and aqua veins that seemed to lie on the top of her hand and converge at her wrist. When she tightened the grip on Cora's hand, Dexter watched her delicate hand bones move.

Cora opened her eyes and for the first time the woman removed her glasses.

"Cora," she aid, "it's me, Jane." Cora smiled and her eyes widened.

"You're getting as light-headed as me," she said, touching the woman's blond hair and then her own close-cropped, white hair.

"What are you doing here, child?"

"I came to see you, Cora."

"When I put you on that bus, you said you was never coming back."

"I lied."

"Don't be lying to me. That bus was over fifteen years ago."

"Seventeen."

"We getting old."

"Speak for yourself."

"Where are my manners?" Cora said, acknowledging the others in the room. "This is Jane Baker, she a pretty famous writer. She's done published three books and sold two movies to Hollywood, haven't you, baby?" Jane nodded and blushed at the praise. Cora continued the introductions.

"This is the new reverend at my church, and this is my grandson, Dexter. You remember when his daddy brought him to see me? You was in third or fourth grade." Jane nodded. "And this is Mrs. Walker, she's been so good to me since I got sick. . . ."

"You brought her into this world when the doctor couldn't make it," Jane said.

"How'd you remember that, child?"

With the introductions completed, the reverend excused himself, promising to be back in a few days. Dexter and Mrs. Walker showed him to the front door, and then they returned to the kitchen.

"Do you remember her?" Dexter asked Mrs. Walker.

"I do now. She was from poor white trash. Her mama was a whore, never looked after the child. Cora was always stepping in, getting the child out of trouble." She poured Dexter a cup of coffee.

Cora and Jane had said nothing to each other since the reverend left the room. They were content to hold each other's hands as the memories spun in their heads. Finally, each came to a point of rest on the memory of their first meeting some thirty years before. Cora spoke first. "I remember the first time I saw you.

"It was about dark when you ran past. I was taking the shortcut. You was at the top of the steps banging on the door calling for your mama. She came but she didn't open the screen. Then that man came. He opened that screen and then sent you tumbling down them steps. Lord, I can still remember the sound you made hitting them steps. She came to see about you, and I thought sure she would take you in, but instead, she shut you in that woodshed. It was dark as pitch when they went back in the house.

"I didn't see no point in letting you stay in that shed all night. I didn't know if you'd come with me, but you did. You climbed into my arms and off we went. When I got you home and turned on the lights, I saw you for the first time. You was dirty and bruised. You kept looking all around.

"I fixed you a bath and put in some bubble soap. You liked them bubbles. I put you in an undershirt and tied it around your middle and fed you some supper. You ate until I thought you'd pop. With all them men around, I guess she had little time to feed you. I held you in my lap and read from the Bible, but you didn't last three verses.

"Then I put you down on the sofa and washed your clothes. I patched them overalls with some calico material and pressed them real nice. We had to get up before light. I cooked biscuits and fried some white meat, dressed you, and off we went.

"You was so warm in my arms, and those feet was tough as leather. I set you down in front of that damn shed, opened the door, and put you in. My God, one of the hardest things I ever did was shut that door." Cora turned her head and closed her eyes.

"I remember that day, too," said Jane.

"Some bigger kids had stopped me as I was going home from school. They called Mama a whore. I didn't know what it meant. They pushed me, and I couldn't get away. I fought for a while, but then I just gave up. When I wouldn't fight any more, they threw some rocks at me and left. I thought Mama would understand. I remember calling for her, and I remember her putting me in the shed.

"I had been locked in that shed on more than one occasion. When you came for me, I thought maybe you were God. Your hands were strong, and I felt so safe. When you brought me here, I was amazed. Mama said coloreds were dirty, but this place was so clean. There was a white cloth on the table. And the bubbles in the bathtub. They caught the light and were filled with color. I didn't want to get in because I didn't want to break any of the bubbles. When Mama bathed me, she stood me under the shower. The water was cold or hot, and she rubbed bar soap on me and then jerked me out. I didn't want to get out of the tub, but I wouldn't tell you because I was afraid you would send me away.

"You took a T-shirt and, with a single piece of thread, you gathered the neck so it wouldn't fall off. Then you tied it around my waist with a red satin ribbon. You let me drink two glasses of milk, and you held me and read to me while I sat in your lap.

"You fed me my first hot breakfast. I wanted to live here forever. It was years before I figured out why I couldn't stay with you. That sort of thing wouldn't happen now." As she lay her head on Cora's breasts as she had some thirty years before, Jane fell asleep.

Mrs. Walker was gone. Dexter had been listening to the muffled sound of voices but for some time had heard only silence. Entering the bedroom, he saw Cora and Jane lying side by side on the bed, sleeping. The picture of the two of them made him nervous, and that made him angry. Did he expect the Klan to come marching through the living room? Would it have bothered him so if they had been in Detroit instead of Alabama? If Dexter Junior—Ahmad—had been there, would it have bothered him? He watched them sleep for a few minutes and then went back to the kitchen.

It was midafternoon when Cora and Jane woke. Cora brushed the blond hair away from Jane's face.

"I want you to leave, Jane," Cora said.

"I want to stay with you."

"There was nothing here for you when I put you on that bus seventeen years ago, and there's nothing for you here now. I won't even be here in a while. You promised you'd never come back. Keep it, baby."

"But . . ."

"No. Now reach under my nightstand and hand me those books."

Jane did as she was told. There were two books. The Bible that Cora had read from when Jane was little and a slim volume of short stories, Jane's first book.

"My two favorite books," Cora said with a wink.

"You have one of the five copies I sold," said Jane, and they laughed. Jane opened her book. She remembered when it was published. The dedication read, *To Cora.* Cora took the book from her hands.

"I think I'll have this buried with me, so I'll have something to read. You take this so you'll have something to read." Cora handed Jane the Bible. Inside the cover she had written, *To Jane.*

"Look here," Cora said, opening the Bible. She pulled out a small black-and-white picture that had yellowed with age. "Dexter's daddy took this when they came to see me. There you are. You was a pretty little thing."

Jane had never seen a picture of herself as a child. She had not known that one existed. She looked at the image of the child who was sitting alone in the distance. Jane embraced Cora as though she were still the child in the picture. After a moment, Cora pulled away.

"Go now," Cora said. "Get on that plane and go back to New York. Don't forget the bad that happened here. That's what made you who you are. Don't dwell on it, neither. And don't look back. Remember Lot's wife."

Clutching the Bible and the picture of the child, Jane walked out of Cora's room and back through the kitchen. She nodded toward Dexter but did not speak. As she opened the screen, she stopped for a moment. Her eyes gazed out over the backyard, and she began to speak. Dexter stood up. He couldn't tell whether she was speaking to him or whether she was speaking to the spirit of Cora that had wandered in that kitchen some thirty years before.

"She fixed my lunch every day. Sometimes a sandwich, sometimes a slice of cake or cookies, and there was always a nickel to buy milk. She would slip the bag into my locker, every day like magic. The other kids would lay their nickel on the counter to buy milk, but I always held mine in my hand. Cora would take the nickel and hold my hand for a minute. If it hadn't been for her, there would have been days that I wouldn't have eaten at all."

She walked off the porch and got into the Chevrolet. She sat for a moment and then drove away with the same speed she had driven earlier that day. Clouds of dust filled the air. Dexter stood at the screen and watched it settle on the red clay road.

Why did she stop writing? Maybe she does write but doesn't tell anyone. I was in a sociology class in college and the professor told us about a study with chimpanzees. They tested them and found that they all had the necessary equipment to speak. Their vocal cords allowed for sound and their mental capacity allowed for the distinction between objects; in fact, one scientist had taught a chimp to use sign language. Still, the chimpanzees had no language. After careful analysis of the information, the scientist was asked, "If the chimp has the ability to speak, why doesn't it speak?" The scientist pondered the question for a moment, and answered, "Maybe it doesn't have anything to say." My professor asked us on his final exam, "Why don't chimps talk?"

I want Jane to write again, but maybe she doesn't have anything left to say.

I want to make love again.

I have never read *The Remains of the Day*.

I never kissed Rudolf Nureyev.

I want to fuck a *Time* cover. Ned Rorem has been to bed with four *Time* covers so far. He still has time. There were three thousand other anonymous souls in Ned's bed. I suppose if you sleep with a thousand people you're bound to increase the chances of fucking a *Time* cover. I have read all of Rorem's diaries and finished his first memoir. I will miss those that follow like I will miss the sound of a *Slow Piece for Cello and Piano*.

I always wanted to learn to play the cello. We say those phrases like we mean them, but do we? If it had really mattered, if I had really wanted to play the cello, wouldn't I have picked up the bow?

I want to make love in the tender and delicate way that Truman Capote put words on the page in *Other Voices, Other Rooms*, lilting and lyrical and precise.

I want to fuck raw and bloody in a fashion that would make Kathy Acker put pen to paper.

I want to remember what it was like to hold someone in my arms and to have them hold me. The pressure of the weight of another body on top of me, the pulling and kneading of fingers and hands, the taste of another mouth, the sound of another heartbeat, I want to write sex on my body, on my page. Mostly, I would like to be able to read one simple passage from Alina Reyes's *The Butcher* or one story from the exacting hand of Angela Carter. If I can imagine it, I can do it, *Time* cover or not.

Cordelia. Cordelia, it's Gabrielle."

"When is your baby due?"

"In three weeks. I'll be out for a while, but you'll have a new nurse who can give shots just as good as I can."

"I don't think I'll need a new nurse."

"Sure you will. She can give you the shots and I can bring the baby by to see you."

"It could be a 'he.' "

"The baby?"

"No, the nurse. Don't be so gender specific. What if the baby wants to be a doctor and she's a girl, or a nurse if he's a boy? You're not going to program this child before it has a chance to even know who it is."

"I love it when you're so political."

"I'm not political, I'm practical. It's the turn of the century, for God's sake. How are things going to ever change."

"Are you in much pain?"

"How come when I'm coherent you always think I'm in pain? When I'm quiet, you think I'm blissful."

"I do not. But I am here to give you a shot."

"I really don't hurt. Give the shot to someone else."

"Sorry, Cordelia, it's all yours. I'll find a strong vein."

"The only thing strong you'll find on me."

"Here's a good one. Take a deep breath. What's the capital of Somalia?"

"I don't—"

"Mogadishu. The capital of Sweden?"

"Stockholm."

"The capital of Botswana?"

"Mogadishu."

"No. That's Somalia."

"I like Mogadishu. It feels good in my mouth. Mogadishu. Would you like to know when you're going to die?"

"What? Everyone dies."

"Yes, but what if you could know exactly when it would come? Would you do it? Know the time? Would it take away the anxiety or make it worse?"

"I don't know. I think I'd want to be surprised."

"My great-aunt knew exactly when it would happen. Susanna. Aunt Susanna. She knew. Her father told her."

"How did he know?"

"He was already dead. My grandmother told me the story.

She got the letter. That was the fifth Cordelia."

"Cordelia. Cordelia, I'll be back tomorrow."

Susanna stood in the kitchen looking out the window at the red Alabama clay that stained her children's feet as they walked barefoot on the roads of Equality. She began to make biscuits in the wooden biscuit bowl she used every day. Resting in a special space on the counter, the bowl was filled with lumpy white flour. Taking her fist, she made an indentation, poured in milk, added a dollop of shortening, and a pinch of salt and soda. She worked the mixture into a ball, kneaded the dough, and rolled it out on the counter. The jelly jar in the cabinet served as biscuit cutter. After laying the soft white circles on the baking sheet, she placed them in the oven. A familiar voice distracted her.

"Susanna."

She recognized her father's voice and turned toward it.

"Susanna, I want you to come with me." Her father stood on the other side of the counter that divided the kitchen from the living room. He looked the way she had always remembered him looking, tall and strong with ragged overalls, cotton shirt, and a bandanna in his pocket. His hands were rough and gnarled from years of trying to support a family from a small parcel of hard ground. Once again his voice drew her toward him.

"I want you to come with me."

"Not today, Dad," she said. "There's a revival at the church and the preacher's all the way from St. Louis. After the revival, then I'll go."

"I'll be back in a week," he said.

Susanna turned back to check the biscuits in the oven. The soft round medallions had risen, turning a crisp golden brown. She laid the steaming bread on a plate and buttered them for the children to eat when they came in after school. When she turned back with the plate, her father had disappeared.

There was little to make this day different from the hundreds of other days, with the exception of her father's reappearance. She had been closer to him than any of her brothers and sisters. Hardly a day passed that she didn't think of him. She saw him in her son's face, she thought of him when the smoke rose from the chimney on a cold day, and when she used the fishing pole he gave her for Christmas, and though he had been dead for nearly seven years, his appearance to her seemed quite normal.

It seemed as though the sun had just risen when Thaddeus and Augusta came in from school the next day.

"Where's the day gone?" Susanna said as she hugged the children. Thaddeus was tall and slim, his boots easily visible at the bottom of his baggy overalls. His blond hair caught the light and was as bright as he was. Though he was younger than his classmates, having skipped the third and fourth grades, he held his own with the other seventh graders.

Augusta was not so fortunate. Small and frail, she had dark straight hair that was short and uneven due to a haircut her mother had given her using a mixing bowl as a guide. It had done little to improve her appearance. While Thaddeus was skipping grades, Augusta was doing her best just to pass, studying hard while her brother breezed through his lessons and went to play. They were good children, but Susanna believed children should be spanked every day to keep them right with God. Thaddeus, with age, had grown wise to Susanna's philosophy, often telling his sister, "You might as well do something bad. Momma's going to whip you anyway." He spoke those very words the day he took his mother's scissors to school.

Susanna prized her sewing scissors. They were small enough to fit in the palm of your hand. The finger holes were gold with leaf designs carved into them. The cutting blades were silver, and when held to the light, not a glimmer could be seen between the blades. They were sharp, both at the point and on the cutting edge. Susanna used them for her tatting and crocheting. No one else was allowed to use them.

Everyone in Thaddeus's class admired the scissors. The forbidden status made them magical. They glided through paper, cutting hundreds of snowflakes. When school ended, the magical scissors, like Cinderella at the stroke of midnight, were sewing scissors once again. As he walked home from school facing a daily spanking, Thaddeus felt in his pocket where the point of the scissors pricked his finger, as if to warn him. He removed the scissors and slipped them into Augusta's knapsack without her noticing.

He and Augusta entered the house and laid their bags on the table. Susanna hugged them and gave them glasses of milk. As Thaddeus finished his last swallow of milk, he began the conversation.

"Mother, ask Augusta what she took to school today."

"What, dear?" Susanna asked the puzzled Augusta. She had no answer, so Thaddeus offered one for her.

"Your sewing scissors," Thaddeus said.

"I did not!" Augusta was on the verge of tears at the suggestion of her guilt.

"Look in her bag," said Thaddeus.

Susanna pulled the little sack she had made across the table, and grasping it by the bottom, she emptied the contents onto the table. Amid the stubby, tooth-marred pencils, the pieces of paper, the broken crayons held in a bundle by a rubber band, were the scissors.

Augusta, in her panic and confusion, could not add two and two and equal Thaddeus. Susanna took the switch from the mantel and spanked Augusta.

"It's bad enough you took my scissors," said Susanna, "but to lie, too. I can't stand lying."

As Augusta turned, she saw Thaddeus smile. Her pain turned to rage, and grasping the closest object to her, a small wooden box, she hurled it toward him only to miss and break the glass in a picture frame. Susanna emerged from the kitchen to deliver Augusta's second spanking of the day. She was sent to bed without supper. After putting dinner on the table and covering it with a dishcloth, Susanna went to bed, too. Thaddeus ate dinner with his father, and for the first time in recent memory, he went to bed without a spanking.

Breakfast was devoid of the usual chatter. It was shaping up to be a quiet day. Susanna cleaned the house, sweeping and dusting, and she took all the dishes out of the cupboards and washed them. She prepared dinner, fed the family, and put them to bed. Remaining awake, she sat at the table and wrote a letter to her sister, Cordelia. Susanna was several years older than her sister. Cordelia was expecting her first child, Susanna her third. She started to write about the day-to-day events. Instead, she wrote about the meeting with their father. She dipped the pen into the ink, and as she wrote, her small characters seemed to wobble. Recounting the story as calmly as it had happened, she told Cordelia the next time her father came, she would go with him. Susanna waved her hand over the paper to dry the ink and noticed it had stained her finger. After she folded the letter, she stuffed it into the envelope and walked out into the night air and placed the letter into the mailbox, raising the red flag.

During the morning with the children at school and Joshua at work, Susanna found herself in the house alone. She sorted the children's clothes and placed the things they could no longer use in a box earmarked for the church clothing room. She gathered up Augusta's two best dresses, her slip and socks, Thaddeus's only pair of long pants and his cotton shirts, and their underwear, and moved to her room. After she laid their clothes on the bed, she took out Joshua's suit and brushed it off. She separated her clothes from Joshua's and emptied the last two drawers of the dresser. Most of her clothes she placed in the next-to-last drawer, and holding up her favorite paisley dress, she looked into the mirror, then carefully folded it with her clean undergarments and laid it on the right side of the bottom drawer.

She took the other clothes to the wash bucket and stood in the sunshine dragging them up and down the washboard. The mailman picked up her letter to Cordelia and waved as he walked on, leaving nothing. As she hung the clothes on the line, she noticed the lye had eaten the ink stains off her finger.

Frying pies for dessert, she thought of the hundreds of crab apples she had peeled, sliced, cored, and dried on the roof. She thought of the weeks it took to dry the apples, and wondered if all the time was worth the effort to stuff a small pie that would be gone in a minute. Later, when she saw Thaddeus and Augusta with the still-warm pies, she had her answer. After dinner she took the clean clothes and ironed for several hours. They looked new, even though they were handed down. Folding the children's clothes, she placed them in the bottom dresser drawer next to the paisley dress.

Friday was always special, the last day of school before the weekend. This Friday the revival was starting, and family and friends would gather from miles around. Susanna told the children, "This preacher has come all the way from St. Louis, Missouri, to bring us the word of God. Come home right after school." She had been looking forward to this revival for several months.

Susanna had Joshua and the children at the church before the doors were open. They sat in the second pew looking up at the pulpit. Susanna's eyes were fixed on the empty cross at the back of the sanctuary. Thaddeus and Augusta fidgeted as though the service would never start. When it did, the church was packed, the choir sang, prayers were said, and then the preacher from St. Louis, Missouri, mounted the pulpit, his voice filling the little church. His sermon moved from salvation to damnation, and then he was screaming. His eyes were on fire, his face reddened, and his finger seemed to be pointing at Augusta, who moved closer to Thaddeus.

Susanna listened intently. The preacher wound to a close and the choir began to sing "Just As I Am," Augusta's favorite hymn, for it always signaled the beginning of the end of the church service. The St. Louis preacher moved to the altar rail and called all sinners forward. He stopped the choir after one verse of the song and began to speak again. He was reserved as the music of the pipe organ swirled in the church. As his voice began to rise, pulsing with the music, he called the lost to the lamb.

It was an awkward moment since no one wanted to be the first sinner to come forward. Thaddeus diverted his eyes from the preacher for the first time that evening and looked at Susanna, whose face was pale and translucent in the light, like the face of an angel. Suddenly Thaddeus grabbed his sister's hand and down they went to the altar rail. Then Susanna's hands were touching Augusta's shoulder and Joshua was standing behind Thaddeus. Everyone in the congregation congratulated the converts. Susanna was so proud of the children that she relived the moments at the altar many times that night before exhaustion forced her to bed.

The newly converted Thaddeus, filled with piety, left the house early in the morning to volunteer to clean the church. Augusta reacted differently, spending her morning playing in the yard. In the afternoon she helped her mother cook for the potluck supper. Her mother cooked in the little kitchen every day, but Augusta had never really watched her before.

Susanna's fingers were long and slender, and they moved through the dough with the grace and deftness of a sculptor. Several times she stopped her work to sit down and rest. During one break she reached out and pulled Augusta close and hugged her. Augusta held her mother's hands, which were dusted with flour and trembled slightly. She ran her small fingers down Susanna's delicate fingers. The excitement over the revival had tired Susanna, and Augusta asked her to rest tonight and save her strength for Sunday morning.

Eighty miles away, Cordelia sat down to read the mail. She sorted the letters, coming to the one with Susanna's handwriting. The writing was sloppy as though Susanna was hurried when she wrote it. She looked forward to Susanna's letters, chatty tales of the children, the people around her, an occasional recipe or poem, fond remembrances of their girlhood.

She tore open the envelope and started to read. The letter began, "Dad came to see me yesterday." Susanna's writing was so natural and honest that for a moment Cordelia could see her father in the present tense. She checked the envelope and found that it was not a long-lost correspondence finally delivered, but a current postmark.

Again, she read the opening line, "Dad came to see me yesterday." No news of the children or the church. She continued reading the story and found that it was not a fond recollection. "Dad came to see me yesterday." She touched her distended belly and folded the letter, holding it a moment before laying it on the shelf. Then she readied her clothes for Sunday's church service.

Susanna had never been happier. She felt the presence of God with her as she sat surrounded by her family at the Sunday-morning church service. The St. Louis preacher had his grand finale, converting people from far and wide. The revival had been a huge success, and as they departed the church, Susanna shook the preacher's hand.

"I'm so glad you came," Susanna said. He patted her hands and kissed them.

"Your mother is a fine woman," the preacher told her children.

Susanna didn't eat Sunday dinner. She lay in her room. Joshua fixed the children's plates and set them at the table. He stayed with Susanna while the children ate. The conversation from the bedroom was muffled.

"It's been the most wonderful week," Susanna said.

"I'll get the doctor from Alex City," said Joshua.

"There's no need."

"What will I do?"

"The children's clothes are in the bottom drawer, and so is my paisley dress."

Joshua had bought her that dress.

"The first time I saw you, you were just thirteen and peeling apples on your father's porch. I noticed your hands before I saw your face. Beautiful hands. They should have had an easy life, not this. I promised your father I would take care of you."

"It won't be long now." Susanna's voice was faint.

"No," said Joshua.

"Get the children," Susanna said. Joshua, who sat on the bed holding her hands, rose and called the children to the bedroom. They climbed on the bed, and Joshua closed the door and waited in the kitchen.

"I'm very proud of both of you," Susanna said. "I want you to take care of your father."

Both children nodded. They talked about Sunday school and dinner and whether snow would come before Christmas. Thaddeus did not look at his mother. Augusta fiddled with the afghan on the foot of the bed, sticking her fingers in and out of the yarn holes. Susanna had wanted to teach her to make the soft shells and string them together into an afghan. She suddenly felt her daughter would never learn to crochet. Augusta quit pulling at the yarn shells, smoothing them gently and refolding the corner. Susanna hugged the children and sent them out to play.

Susanna turned and looked out the window. Her father sat in the rocker on the porch.

"I'm ready, Dad," said Susanna.

The telegram came early Monday morning. Cordelia was still in her dressing gown when it was delivered. She thanked the boy and laid the yellow envelope on the counter. She did not have to open it. She sat at the table and pulled Susanna's letter off the shelf. Touching her hand flat to the page, she looked at the frail writing between her fingers. She held the page up to the light.

"Dad came to see me yesterday." Cordelia reread the letter several times.

$\mathcal{M}$y grandmother Cordelia read the letter. I asked her once if she kept the letter from Susanna. She hadn't seen any point to it. It is one of those objects you have always heard about and desperately want to possess. For years I thought that maybe one day I would find it in a box, tossed aside. I would be looking for something else and there in a tattered envelope would be Susanna's letter. I never found it, but can't help wishing I had the letter written in Susanna's hand.

Letters are not always something one keeps. As I think back on it now, there are many letters I wish I had kept. I love reading letters, my own and other people's. Virginia Woolf kept scores of letters. Think how wonderful they are to read. All of Virginia's letters arranged in volume after volume. There are the letters of Virginia to Vita Sackville-West, a correspondence of a friendship and more. There are only Violet Trefusis's letters to Vita left. Violet's husband destroyed all of Vita's letters, as if burning the paper they were written on would destroy their feelings for each other. Theirs were the letters of children enamored of each other, of friends and of lovers, but Vita's are gone. Susanna's are gone. I have Brian's last postcard with the *Isenheim Altarpiece* on the front and GOOD-BYE on the back. I have a flowered box filled with letters from a friend, a lover, a confidante—all of Sasha's letters that were ever addressed to me sit in the box. And what of my letters? Gone, I'm sure. She is not the type to keep such sentimental attachments.

Vita's letters gone.

Susanna's letters gone.

My letters gone.

Why does anyone even bother to write letters today? The telephone has robbed us of the simple, elegant way to communicate, to express feelings, to love, and to lie. The silky feel of the paper, the smell of the ink, the taste of the stamp, gone with the push of a telephone number. Some say the fax will bring back letter writing as a popular pastime. A marvel of the modern age—the more things change, the more they stay the same.

My darling,

I was enjoying the melancholy pleasure of looking through your letters this evening, when it occurred to me that it has been some time since I had had one from you—not, in fact, since I was in Berlin. And now you are in London, and you won't have time to write. Besides, if I have not had letters from you it is because I have been with you, which is better than ink and paper.

*C*ordelia remembers the letters of other people. She has read more letters addressed to other people than one could imagine. All the letters of Virginia, Vita, and Violet in various forms by various editors.

> Henry Miller's to Lawrence Durrell
> Simone de Beauvoir's to Jean-Paul Sartre
> Max Perkins's to Scott Fitzgerald
> Philip Larkin's
> Flannery O'Connor's
> Lillian Smith's
> Edith Wharton's
> Elizabeth Bishop's
> Paul Bowles's

Cordelia wonders sometimes if perhaps the letters are not too intimate. Would one write a letter knowing that forty years later an absolute stranger would read it? A letter read out of context with no preceding letter, or response? Would you write a letter filled with the intimate details of your life and post it to someone you loved knowing that the letter would find its way into a book long after you were dead? Most people never imagine their letters in a book, but Cordelia sees everything in terms of books and words. Now she worries about the small points because she has no more large points to worry about. All the big decisions have been made in her life, and she worries about little things, old things, memories to keep her mind off the pain. She worries about the letters that she never sent—and she worries about the letters that were sent.

Dear Cordy,

Welcome back! How was your voyage? I would love to hear! Are you in a quiet mood these days? How are you?

I've been hibernating. Working very hard on my new book and an enormous article I have coming out in the *Atlantic*. It's been exhausting. In the next few months I must finish this novel. For entertainment I've been writing erotic études. You would love them. I'll send some on. I am wishing for snow. It would help me to concentrate.

Thanks for the book you sent. It was very sweet. Have you read it? I must say I am afraid she is losing her touch. What trouble she must be in. I worry for her.

Do write a long letter and tell me how things are for you. Are you writing? Are you busy? Are you in Alabama much?

I hope this finds you well,

Sasha

I think the cello is the most feminine musical instrument. I want to learn to play the cello, but I don't have time. I love Bach's cello concertos and Vivaldi's. I enjoy Yo-Yo Ma, but I prefer that the cello be played by a woman, Jacqueline duPré or Jane Scarpantoni or Ofra Harnoy. The cello reminds me of the female body, the way the female body should be, compact and curvy, with a deep, rich sound. In order to play the cello, one has to hold and caress the instrument and fawn over it as the bow gently coaxes a sound. And what a sound it can make, painfully poetic or bold and exaggerated. The cello sounds like a woman, a woman who has lived life and enjoyed every minute of it.

Vivaldi composed twenty-seven cello concertos. My favorite is the "Concerto in G Major." It can blow the *Four Seasons* right out of the water. It has a slow movement filled with the poetry of a magical lamentation. The beauty of the rich cello surrounded by the harpsichord and strings is as exquisite as any musical score could possibly be. The cello is an instrument for an angel, an angel with strong hands and tender thighs.

allons danser . . .

*C*ordelia, I'm going to set the food right here. Can I feed you?"

"No. I'm all right."

"How are you doing today?"

"I'm all right."

"I brought in your mail. Junk, mostly. Catalogues—Victoria's Secret, Totally Tomatoes."

"Totally Tomatoes is my favorite. Only tomatoes and peppers. I look forward to it. I order the newest tomato and the hottest peppers."

"You like tomatoes, do you?"

"Actually, I hate tomatoes. But I grow them. It's a cultural thing. Decrepit old Southern ladies growing tomatoes. I grow them and let them rot on the vine. Maybe this is a cosmic payback."

"What? You want me to put on a movie? You got more movies than anyone I know. It's like a video store. Let's see. Don't you have any films by Americans? Gee, I never heard of most of these guys."

"There are some in English. I can't see the subtitles anymore."

"Everything's in black and white."

"Nothing is in black and white."

"What? How about *Queen Christina?*"

"Did you know Katherine Anne Russell?"

"Yes, I did. She was quite a character. A real old-fashioned lady, but I hear in her younger days she was quite a rounder. Who knows, though. She's been dead for years now. Died before your grandmother did, didn't she? Miss Katherine Anne, what a character."

"I wrote about her once when I was a boy."

"When you were a boy? You're a little confused about that, aren't ya, Cordelia?"

"I can be anybody on the page."

$\mathcal{K}$atherine Anne Russell was the Greta Garbo of Equality. Countless stories circulated about her when I was a child. She remained reticent, content to spend most of her time inside the Russell house. When she did venture outside, immaculately dressed with a stylish hat and white gloves, the whole town talked about the event for days. I hadn't thought of Miss Katherine Anne for years, until Aunt Cordelia sent me a chocolate pound cake in the mail. Stuffed around the wrapped cake to prevent sliding were several crumpled pages from the county newspaper. In the lower right-hand corner of the front page was an old picture of Miss Katherine Anne as she appeared at her coming-out party in 1942. Beside the picture was her obituary.

In the gigantic myth that surrounded Miss Katherine Anne, there are some stories that have survived the years and are partly true, and there are some stories that I know to be true because I was there. Miss Katherine Anne had spent her formative years on the verandahs of Montgomery, attending dancing classes, piano lessons, and proper teas. Several times she had accompanied her parents to New York City on the train. She had been in the midst of a brilliant social season at the Montgomery Country Club when fate, or more precisely, the philandering and subsequent departure of her father, changed all that.

Returning home one evening from a ball where every young army officer would have relinquished his commission just to have danced with Miss Katherine Anne, she found her dashing father had dashed out of town with a young woman of questionable social standing and had taken with him the contents of the family bank account. He left behind a Croix de Guerre from World War I and a flask inscribed, "BEST WISHES," FROM F. SCOTT. Within days, Miss Katherine Anne and her mother were on the doorstep of her uncle, Thomas Parker Russell. Within weeks her mother expired of a nondescript ailment, often described as a broken heart, but from a medical standpoint, it was probably complications from syphilis. The death thrust Mr. Russell and Miss Katherine Anne together in a most unholy alliance.

Thomas Parker Russell was unequipped to deal with a seventeen-year-old belle from Montgomery. He had been somber even as a child. He graduated from military school and left behind his socially prominent family to open a mill in Equality. In the years to come he prospered, acquiring the hardware store, the newspaper, the casket factory, and most important, the bank. Owning the mill and the bank was like owning Park Place and Boardwalk. Thomas Parker Russell had cornered the game.

He resided in a large white house with a screened-in porch on the lot at the end of Main Street. The house was acquired in a foreclosure. His bank held ninety-nine cents of every dollar he made. The suits he wore had belonged to his father. He had salvaged them from the charity box upon his father's death, and though they were out of style, they served his purpose. In spring and summer he ate one boiled brown egg for breakfast, in fall and winter a bowl of oatmeal with milk and no sugar. He drank a cup of tea at noon and at night, each brewed with the same tea bag. When Old Man Russell and Miss Katherine Anne sat face to face under the same roof, sparks flew.

Miss Katherine Anne was supposed to go to Agnes Scott, a

women's college in Georgia, but her uncle was of the impression that women need not be educated and decided that she should go to work in his bank. Work was a foreign concept to Miss Katherine Anne, and she was devastated to find herself behind a desk. After six months in Equality, Miss Katherine Anne was in need of some excitement. Just how much excitement she found has been debated for years.

I had heard much whispering about her, and finally my grandmother told me that Miss Katherine Anne was a fallen woman who had gone off by herself with two boys. The facts are a bit more scattered. One night after work, Miss Katherine Anne was offered a ride home by Dickie Reed and Calvin Jakes. Dickie's father was the undertaker and Calvin's father was the only doctor in Equality. Both had gotten out of serving in the war, Dickie because he was an only child and Calvin because of a self-inflicted gunshot wound. There was little doubt that she went riding with them, but I know that Miss Katherine Anne was far too worldly to have been impressed by Dickie's stories of the involuntary movements of corpses or of Calvin's aspirations to brain surgery.

There was no evidence to indicate that the evening consisted of anything more than a ride home, unless you heard the story from Dickie and Calvin. Within a week the two boys had transformed a charming Southern belle into a hussy who had slept with the entire University of Alabama football team and the Auburn defense. Miss Katherine Anne took the gossip in stride, but she never forgot who had started the rumors. Thirty-five years would pass before the opportunity for revenge would present itself, and I was to be the catalyst for that revenge.

After all that time, Equality was still a small Southern town with many of the same names and faces. The war in Vietnam was taking the sons of the boys who had fought World War II. There was racial unrest and student unrest that escaped Equality. Old Man Russell had gotten frail and was unable to work, and the job of running both the mill and the bank fell to Miss Katherine Anne. She was the most powerful woman in Equality; yet people still spoke of her scarlet past in hushed voices, and children who weren't even born in 1942 could recite the most intimate details of that joyride.

Calvin Jakes had not accomplished his dream of brain surgery, settling instead on a career as the town pharmacist. Calvin's new ambition was to be mayor of Equality, a position he saw as a stepping stone to the governor's mansion. Calvin had grown portly with age. His hair was falling out, and when the light hit the bald spot, Calvin looked like an airport beacon. Every time I went into his drugstore, I thought about him in the car with Miss Katherine Anne and cold chills ran all over me. I just knew that such a refined lady would have never done anything bad with Calvin, much less the undertaker's son.

One fall day in the middle of an Indian summer, I entered Calvin's drugstore in search of candy. I had only four cents in my pocket. Calvin was talking politics and was so involved with trying to get votes that he had little time to run the store. The only way to get his attention was to offer him a silver dollar, a coin he'd been collecting for years. Many silver dollars were on display, and a sign hung over the cash register offering two paper dollars for any one silver dollar. I rubbed the four pennies in my pocket and thought about all the Hershey bars I could buy if just one of those pennies were a silver dollar.

I could have bought some gum or jawbreakers, but I had my heart set on a Hershey Bar. Calvin wasn't paying any attention to me as I searched the candy rack. I picked up the Hershey Bar several times, smelling the aroma of chocolate. Finally, I took the bar in my hand, turned, and headed for the door. I almost fainted when I saw Miss Katherine Anne standing before me. I wondered if she had watched me take the candy, but I didn't have time to think. I never made it outside. Before I could reach the door, Calvin grabbed my shoulders.

"What you got there, child?" he said.

There was nothing I could say. Calvin entered into a soapbox speech about law and order that I thought lasted an hour, though in my nervous state it had probably been only minutes. By one small lapse of judgment, I had become a criminal and single-handedly elected Calvin Jakes mayor. Everybody in the store was looking at me. While I stared at the floor, I noticed Miss Katherine Anne's feet beside mine. As I looked up, her hat shielded me from the mob that had gathered, and for the first time, I heard her speak.

"We must teach responsibility," she said in a refined voice that was a full octave lower than Calvin's. Calvin seized her remark, damning me again to a packed house. Miss Katherine Anne kept nodding in agreement as I became the biggest criminal since Al Capone.

"You're such an honorable man, Calvin," she went on. "Don't you often let the children just leave their candy money on the counter and trust them to be honest?"

Calvin jumped on this compliment with a vengeance, extolling his virtue as a shopkeeper and leader in the community.

"Well," Miss Katherine Anne said, drawing the word to several syllables. "Isn't that the child's dime sitting right there on your counter?"

Everyone followed Miss Katherine Anne's gloved hand as she pointed to the shiny dime lying in plain view on the counter. Calvin was speechless and so was I; after all, I only had four cents, and I didn't leave a one of them on the counter. Miss Katherine Anne tore into Calvin.

"How could you accuse such a sweet child of stealing, Calvin? You're supposed to be a leader in this community." Calvin's head hung lower and lower as he saw his campaign for mayor melting like my Hershey Bar.

"If it were me, Calvin, I would give this child another candy bar and one of those silver dollars you're so proud of and hope that he doesn't call a lawyer or the police."

Calvin followed her instructions to the letter, and then Miss Katherine Anne escorted me outside into the autumn air.

Standing on the corner, just out of view of the drugstore window, Miss Katherine Anne removed both candy bars and the silver dollar from my hands. She glared down at me, lowering the brim of her hat in such a way that I could not see her eyes.

"You shouldn't steal," she said.

I don't know what came over me, but I looked up at where I thought her eyes might be and mustered all my courage.

"You shouldn't lie, either." I could have died. I knew she was going to do something terrible to me, and I was imagining what it would be, when I heard her laugh. She slipped the silver dollar into her pocket and handed me one of the Hershey bars. Then she took the remaining bar and opened the wrapper and began to eat it without getting one speck of chocolate on her white gloves.

"You owe me a favor. One day I'll collect."

As the years passed, the taste of chocolate always made me think of Calvin's election loss and of Miss Katherine Anne. I was convinced that after eight years she had forgotten the favor, though she never saw me on the street without speaking. She would wait until we had just passed each other and then she would say hello, causing me to turn around and look at her only to see the back of her dress and the brim of her hat. It had been eight years since the incident in Calvin's drugstore and two years since old Thomas Parker Russell had died at the ripe old age of ninety-three.

I had become quite popular and was always surrounded by giggling girls. One day as I stood on the corner showing off, I barely noticed Miss Katherine Anne walk by, but she noticed me.

"You owe me a favor. Be at my house Saturday morning at nine. Wear your Sunday suit." With those words, she was gone.

I was somewhat scared by the summons and somewhat thrilled that I owed a favor to the elusive Katherine Anne Russell. Despite my apprehensions, I was at her house as the Methodist Church bells began to strike nine. No one that I knew of had ever been inside the Russell house. Miss Katherine Anne met me at the door. It was the first time that I had seen her without gloves or a hat, and I looked away as though she were standing there stark naked.

"At least you're on time," she said.

The house was as I had imagined it, filled with old expensive furniture and books. Dark and lonely. We sat at the dining room table, and she served tea. As she handed me a cup, I couldn't help but look at her hands. They were not the hands of a woman her age, they were smooth and manicured, a result of all those years in gloves.

"Read this," she said, as she handed me a folded paper that read REED FUNERAL HOME on the outside. As I began to read, I found that the document was a burial policy for Thomas Parker Russell, but couldn't for the life of me figure out why I was reading it.

"Well, you're a smart boy. What does it say?"

I really didn't know what she wanted.

"Read this paragraph, here."

The paragraph in question stated that Reed Funeral Home would bury the deceased in a casket that they would guarantee against leakage for five years, or they would replace the casket and refund your money.

"How would anyone know?" she asked.

"You'd have to dig it up, but no one would do that."

I looked up at Miss Katherine Anne, and she was smiling.

"Let's go," she said, and off we headed to see Dickie Reed.

Dickie was somewhat shocked to see Miss Katherine Anne on the arm of such a young escort. He took us into his office and chatted to us in a condescending voice. At Miss Katherine Anne's instruction, I handed him the policy.

"I want to check it for leakage, Dickie," she told him.

Dickie began to sweat. He'd never heard of such a thing. The clause was in the contract just to protect the loved ones. He knew that no one would ever use the clause, but then he hadn't counted on Miss Katherine Anne.

"My uncle was a thrifty man, Dickie. He always stuck to a contract, and I want to see that you stick to this one."

Dickie was between a rock and a hard place, a place where no one wanted to be stuck with Miss Katherine Anne. I think Dickie was clinging to the hope that the casket had lived up to the claim in the burial policy, as he had the backhoe dig into the grave. I also think that he was convinced that somehow nobody would find out about this, but in Equality, digging up a grave in broad daylight receives a great deal of attention.

Dickie jerked and fidgeted as the backhoe dug deeper. Miss Katherine Anne stood still and erect as the cemetery filled with curious townspeople. When the backhoe hit five feet, Dickie almost fainted, but there was no place to fall as the cemetery was filled with spectators. The next shovel of dirt was accompanied by a piece of casket that resembled an old cardboard box left in the rain. Miss Katherine Anne looked into the grave and then at Dickie.

"My uncle needs a new casket, Dickie, and a check for his policy." With that we walked through the crowd back to the funeral home.

Within an hour the moldy remains of Thomas Parker Russell were resting in a fine cherry wood casket. Top of the line. A vault had been hastily set into the grave. A devastated Dickie Reed, his hands shaky and sweating, signed over the amount of the burial policy to Miss Katherine Anne.

"It's time to bury my uncle," she said to Dickie, and I walked her back to the cemetery with Dickie in tow like a scolded puppy. The cemetery was filled to overflowing. Three times as many people were in attendance for this burial of Thomas Parker Russell as there had been at the first burial. As we approached the cemetery, the crowd parted to let Miss Katherine Anne stand beside the grave. The crowd grew quiet as the wooden coffin was lowered into the vault. Several people in the crowd noted that Old Man Russell would have been real proud of his niece. It was indeed a fitting final farewell.

Walking back to the Russell house, I realized that after forty-three years, Miss Katherine Anne was even. I was proud to have accompanied her to this funeral, and I was glad that I had stolen that Hershey Bar from Calvin. I wanted to say something to her as we approached the house, but I didn't know what to say. She didn't speak to me. I hated for the day to end in silence, but the words escaped me.

She walked up the stairs, and I turned to leave. I turned back as she called my name. Her hand was thrust into her pocket as she smiled at me.

"We're even, now," she said as her hand rose from her pocket, pitching something toward me. I followed the arc of her hand and watched as the sun hit the object in midair, causing it to glow. I caught it. Opening my hand, I saw the eagle sitting erect on the silver dollar that Calvin had given me eight years ago. When I looked up, she had already disappeared into the house.

*M*iss Katherine Anne is gone now. Garbo is gone. Gone but not forgotten.

> Cordelia,
> I know you're faking this sick thing. Get the fuck back to New York. Trust me! You'll feel better. Please come back.
>
> Matthew

Matthew keeps sending me irreverent postcards begging me to come back to the city. He always writes "fuck" on the cards but he never said the word to me, not after I said the word cancer to him. He knows that I won't be coming back, but he believes if he keeps sending the postcards, he can keep me alive. Everyone has his own game associated with my dying. I had a mover come in and pack up all the fiction in my bedroom. I kept all the fiction together on shelves that lined an entire wall. The books were alphabetized, and often when we would lie in bed, Matthew would tease me about my books. I would tell him that when he died, I wanted all his Black Sparrow editions of Paul Bowles. He said he would come to my house and get all the Kate Bravermans, especially the first book where she was Katherine Braverman. He wanted my *Other Voices, Other Rooms*. I wanted his copy of Katherine Dunn's *Truck*. I wanted his Jargon Society edition of Lorine Niedecker poetry. We argued over how to pronounce her name—NI-decker, NEE-decker, ni-DECKER, we never knew. The movers packed the books in alphabetized boxes

Acker–Auster
Auther–Barnes, Djuna
Barnes, Julian–Colwin
Cortazar–Davenport
Dillard–Faulkner

and on and on. . . . Twenty-eight boxes of fiction shipped to his small, fourth-floor walk-up. Boxes were stacked everywhere. I sent him a note.

Matthew,
  Be careful what you wish for—it might come true. Here is Kate Braverman's first book back when she was a young Katherine Braverman, and a few more. Many of them are signed, but you'll have to find them. Leave no title page unturned. I wish one of them had my name on the title page. *C'est la vie.* Or maybe not. Enjoy! Enjoy them as I have enjoyed being with you.
                    All the love that's left,

                    Cordelia

*M*en don't handle death well. Cordelia says it's woman's work, like childbirth and cleaning. It isn't that Matthew doesn't care about Cordelia; it's just that he doesn't know how to handle it. The lover thing hadn't worked out that well. There was love but no real passion, and they were both cursed with hopeless romanticism. The lack of passion didn't keep them out of bed with each other, but it was a given that it wouldn't last forever; in fact, it only lasted until the next big crush came along. It resumed after one of them was crushed, and they vowed to remain best friends. Matthew's last crush seemed pretty crushed on him. They were in the throes of mutual crushdom when Cordelia packed for Alabama.

Dying in Equality is a family tradition, she told him. No doctor from New York or any other new place can help me. I'm going home. I'll have my memories and you'll have Rebecca. You're happy, so it will be a good time to go. They had a good-bye dinner at 21, a place they had always wanted to go but could never afford. They toasted the good times over caviar and champagne. He kissed her good-bye. Good-bye was all he could say.

Perhaps he would have handled it better if he had been gay. Gay men understand the drama of death. Life is like opera. Wayne Koestenbaum wants to die peacefully with opera playing. Or perhaps in a terminal splurge, with a live singer, a student singer, a singer interested in the dying. He says I want to be reminded, when I leave my body, that even when I lived inside it I never fully used it. Matthew is a blatant heterosexual. He wouldn't know where to look for a singer interested in the dying. He wouldn't understand living in a partially used body. A body that never played the cello, never kissed Nureyev, never fucked a *Time* cover, never has been to Spain.

Death is the last great equalizer. Cordelia has made all the plans. There will be no service of any kind. Her body will be cremated and the ashes interred in the family plot. There are three funeral homes in Equality, but none of them cremate on the premises. The body still has to be taken to Montgomery. Cordelia will be the second person in Equality to be cremated.

$\mathcal{B}$obby and Tammy were both white trash. They had been born on the wrong side of the single set of tracks that cut across Equality. Bobby's daddy ran off and so did his stepdaddy, leaving his mother with him and three little ones and barely enough money to buy cigarettes. Tammy's mother died in childbirth, and her father was the town drunk.

Both were bad in school. Bobby played football, and Tammy played hooky. Bobby failed eleventh grade, but the football coach got him into the senior class. Tammy barely passed. Bobby didn't have money for dates. Tammy didn't either. They made love in the backseat of a '48 Chevy for entertainment. In their senior year, Bobby broke the school record for touchdowns and won a football scholarship to Ole Miss. Tammy got pregnant and had a baby. Bobby never came back. Tammy was in Equality forever.

The baby was born in the summer. Tammy was unsure of her body and what to expect from the birth. All she knew of childbirth was that her mother had died from it. Realizing that she was in labor, she went to the clinic. Dr. Campbell poked and prodded and said it would take time. When time came, she thought she was going to die, but the old doctor reassured her. Alone in the delivery room, she cried out not as much in pain as in frustration. As the contractions increased, so did her screaming. The doctor stuck his head into the room at the same time as the baby. Nature had moved faster than Doctor Campbell had anticipated. Sitting up for a final push, she delivered the child. Weakly she watched as the doctor held him aloft by the ankles and smacked the baby who let out a loud cry.

Later, as she lay in a small room in the rear of the clinic, she picked up a book filled with children's names. Turning to the section on boys' names, she began to read. The first name was Aaron. She had never seen a word begin with two *A*s before so she dismissed it as a misprint. The next name was Abraham. It was hard to spell and the only Abraham she knew of was Lincoln. She moved down the list. The next name was Adam. It was short and simple. She named her son Adam.

Doctor Campbell didn't leave the clinic after the delivery. He sat with Adam for a long time. He had delivered almost everyone in Equality for the past thirty-five years. He had delivered children and then their children. Every now and again he delivered a calf or a colt. This baby was different. He had seen it only once or twice in thousands of babies. He could tell when they were special because he saw it so seldom, and he knew that Adam was one of the few. It was as if the boy had been touched by God.

In the years that followed, Adam grew to be a bright and clever child. Tammy got a steady job at the five-and-dime. Her father died, and he was replaced with a new town drunk, lifting his stigma from her shoulders. Other girls got pregnant. The Hobson boy let a Chinaman move into his house on the hill. She and Adam had moved up a rung on Equality's social ladder.

She rented a small house that had once been the slave quarters of the Russell house. She kept the house clean, though there was little furniture. She built some shelves with concrete blocks and boards where she set a picture of Adam and some other trinkets from her past. She salvaged an old set of encyclopedias that had been discarded, probably because volumes Q and Z were missing, and she found that Adam spent a great deal of his time pouring over the books. By the time Adam was eight years old, he had skipped two grades in school. He spent most of his time reading, and his only real friend became the Chinaman who lived on the hill.

There was a great deal of talk about the Chinaman in Equality. The Chinaman's son and the Hobson boy were partners in several Chinese restaurants in Alabama. The Chinaman didn't like Birmingham or Montgomery. He wanted to be in the country, and the Hobson boy let him stay in the house in Equality. He cultivated a small garden and never came into town. Many of Adam's schoolmates thought the Chinaman was a wizard.

"He can put a spell on you, Adam," one kid said, as Adam walked through the five-and-dime where his mother worked.

"You shouldn't let your boy talk to that Chinaman," Rose Wiley said to Adam's mother, as she placed the hair net and face powder into a bag. Rose always spoke her mind, even if she was wrong. Turning to a woman who was in her Sunday school class, Rose said, "I hear that Chinaman does pyrotechnics."

"No!" the startled woman replied.

"I know it to be true."

"Well!"

"And she lets that little boy go up there." Rose looked toward Adam's mother. "Pyrotechnics!"

"Fireworks," Adam said as he stood by his mother and looked up at Rose and her Sunday School friend. "Mr. Lee makes fireworks. That's what pyrotechnics is."

His mother smiled at Adam. Rose Wiley glared at the boy and grabbed her bag off the counter. The Sunday School lady winked at Adam as if she had known all along that pyrotechnics were fireworks. Then she followed Rose out of the store.

Adam knew the Chinaman wasn't a wizard, but seeing all of his pots and jars and powders might make a boy believe in wizards. The Chinaman showed him the black powder, a ground-up mixture of potassium nitrate, sulfur, and charcoal that was the main ingredient in the fireworks. To make colors, the Chinaman explained, you added different chemicals. Sodium salts for yellow. Iron for orange. Strontium salts for red. Barium nitrate for green. White and blue were hard to achieve. Aluminum or magnesium produced a white color. Blue, a bright blue that keeps its deep color, is impossible. The copper salts had to be in the presence of a volatile chlorine donor. Adam watched each day as the Chinaman showed him more about the fireworks.

In the evenings, Adam would tell his mother all about the things he had learned. He told her that Marco Polo was the first to describe firecrackers that were just sections of bamboo thrown on a fire. Each chemical that the Chinaman used had a different smell and look. There were shells the powders went into and a special way to layer the shell for each kind of effect. She would listen to her son, though she never understood what he was talking about. At night they would sit outside and look at the stars.

The first of June, Tammy began to think of a present to give her son for his ninth birthday. She would have to decide before the middle of the month. She searched the shelves of the five-and-dime. On the back shelf sat a large box. It was filled with beakers and vials and little jars labeled aluminum and sodium and sulfur, things that Adam talked about. She was sure he would love the chemistry set, so she bought it.

Three days after Adam's ninth birthday, his mother heard a loud explosion as she worked in the five-and-dime. At first, she thought it was Mr. Lee and his pyrotechnics. Soon she found out the truth. Standing in front of the rented house, unable to get closer, she heard Rose Wiley tell a friend, "She had no business having a child if she wasn't going to look after it." Adam was dead.

The police took her to the house. The windows in the room that had once been Adam's were blown out. The body would be sent to the medical examiner in Montgomery. She would have to go and sign papers. Did she understand? She nodded and sat in the swing on the lawn as boards were nailed over the missing windows on the side of the house.

Tammy sat outside most of the night as people came by to gawk, but not to pay condolences. Entering the house, she went directly to her bedroom and changed clothes, stopping for a moment to rest her hand on the common wall between her room and Adam's.

The bus to Montgomery arrived at the Equality station at 7:31 A.M. The station was the corner in front of the Carter Hardware Store, and when the bus arrived, she boarded and sat in the row behind the driver.

Arriving in Montgomery, she walked to the medical examiner's office and waited for twenty minutes until the office opened. The medical examiner had not expected her to be alone. He tried to be delicate, but delicacy was never a part of the job.

"Have you thought about the funeral? I mean the body. . . . I would suggest cremation." His eyes were hollow. "I can give you the name of the funeral home to do it. I can go ahead and have the body sent there."

The medical examiner expressed his sorrow as he walked her to the door. She took the address and stepped outside into the warm summer air. The twelve-block walk left her exhausted as she climbed the steps to the funeral home. She read the name of the body that lay in Parlor A, and she watched as a steady stream of friends and family filed in and out.

"He's ready now." The soft voice of the funeral director startled her. She had been waiting for five hours. The man stood before her dressed in a dark suit and held out a white box that looked as though it could have been a gift. Hesitantly, she reached out, taking the box from his hands, and cradling it gingerly in her arms, she walked to the bus station and waited for the bus home.

Stepping off the bus, Tammy turned away from her house and walked up the road toward the Hobson place. In the afternoon sun, the dusty, windy road was a difficult climb. As she approached the house, she saw the Chinaman rise from his gardening and come toward her. Adam had spoken often of Mr. Lee, but she had never imagined what he looked like. The small, white-haired man bowed before her. She looked into his eyes and without saying a word, she handed him the box. He smiled and bowed again. She left and returned home to try and sleep.

The red rays of the sunset were shining through the window as she awoke from a restless sleep. She got out of bed, bathed and washed and dried her hair. Under the sink she found her old electric curlers which she had almost forgotten how to use. She put on her underwear and applied her makeup. When she went back into the bedroom, she turned on the light. Rummaging through her drawers, she found an old pair of black tights and she put them on. She slipped into her black high heels and opened the closet to find her only black dress. She pulled on the wool dress, rolling down the turtleneck collar and pushing up the long sleeves. She looked in the mirror and combed her hair again. Then she walked to the front door.

Stepping off the tiny porch, Tammy walked down the two steps and crossed the darkened yard to the swing. As she sat in the swing, she watched the fireflies flicker on and off. In the black sky, she saw a lone star. Star light, star bright, but she knew her one wish could not be answered. Sweat rolled down her back. She could feel steam rising from her body under the weight of the dress. The wool made her feel as if she had wandered into a bed of fire ants. The curl in her hair began to relax as she watched the night sky.

The sudden explosion made her jump as she recalled the events of the last two days. Then there was another and another. The sky was on fire as red and green sparks filled the night above Equality. A whistle shell shrieked through the air, exploding in a yellow light. People came out of their houses to watch as star bursts of blue and green and orange covered the sky. Cars pulled off the road and the streets filled with spectators.

Serpent shells zigzagged across the night as everyone in Equality watched and cheered. The lights were so bright that you could read a candy wrapper. There were some people close to the hill who could feel the heat from the falling sparks. The dazzling display lasted for twenty minutes. Finally, a ball of light tore through the sky, climbing higher and higher. When it reached its zenith, the light hung in the sky for one brief second before exploding into a thousand stars that cascaded to the earth. The exploding stopped but the colors hung in the sky like crayon marks that would not wash away.

I missed *Queen Christina*, but then I've seen it many times. I watched it the day Garbo died. I was in a taxi headed for the Village when they announced it on the radio. I bought some white roses and a pint of Ben & Jerry's New York Super Fudge Chunk and went up to my apartment and pulled out all the Garbo movies I had on tape and I watched them one after another until the morning came.

Queen Christina, directed by Rouben Mamoulian
Anna Christie, directed by Clarence Brown
Camille, directed by George Cukor
Mata Hari, directed by George Fitzmaurice
Ninotchka, directed by Ernst Lubitsch

One of Garbo's lovers was Mercedes de Costa. One of her other lovers was Marlene Dietrich. Dietrich was Mercedes de Costa's lover, giving de Costa the rare privilege of having been the only person to have slept with both women. No one has come forward to challenge her title. Truman Capote invented a game he called "International Daisy Chain." The object of the game was to link two people sexually by the fewest number of beds. Capote said the best card to hold was Mercedes de Costa because with de Costa you could get to anyone from Cardinal Spellman to the Duchess of Windsor. I regret that I will never have sex again, though I think about it often.

Garbo sent de Costa dozens and dozens of white flowers. When de Costa said she had run out of vases to put the flowers in, Garbo sent Lalique.

Olga Broumas was right when she said three in a bed could be nice. Garbo and Dietrich were never in de Costa's bed at the same time, though I am convinced that she pondered the possibility. With sex for two, both people are so involved in the sex act itself, that they fail to have the pleasure of watching their partner. Sex à trois provides that pleasure, the ability to pull away and watch, to see the face in heat of passion, to study the rhythm of the body, to share an orgasm without actually being there. In fact, there are those times when watching someone you love orgasm is a greater thrill than causing them to orgasm. I have had my last orgasm and now all I have is a list of lost ménages à trois.

Jane and Paul Bowles on a rooftop in Tangiers, the moon in

Jane's red hair, Paul playing the piano, wine and kif and a sheltering sky. Dick Cavett and Carrie Nye in their house on Montauk in the bed that came from Carrie Nye's family in Mississippi. Dick would tell witty stories of Jean Stafford and Tennessee Williams and Carrie Nye would laugh a deep Southern laugh as the ocean breeze fluttered the lace curtains. Marianne Faithfull and Mick Jagger in the Chelsea Hotel filled with Jack Daniels and pure heroin and deafening rock and roll. Mercedes de Costa and Ned Rorem, think of the stories. Matthew and Sasha. It would never happen, but they are two people I wouldn't want to live without. I will have to have them alone. And Garbo, I would want to have Garbo alone with white roses in Lalique vases.

$\mathcal{W}$hen the tape goes off the television has an annoying hiss, as though a million cicadas were locked inside. The sound of the cicada is deeply imbedded in the landscape of the South. Lawrence Durrell called it a spirit of place. He felt that landscape was the most often overlooked element in writing. How else, he reasoned, did a universal faith like Catholicism take on such different faces in Italy, in Spain, in Mexico. The South has its own face, the red clay, the magnolias, the cries of the cicada. Cordelia calls them "protracted meeting bugs." She learned the term from her mother, who learned it from her mother. Cordelia was sitting on the porch one hot Alabama afternoon drinking iced tea from a tall glass. A drought had engulfed the South—this being the twenty-seventh day without rain. Normally, the yard is lush with tall stalks of supple grass, each blade standing erect and fighting the crowd to see which one will grow the tallest before being cut short by the lawn mower. Today the lawn is spotted with brown grass. Instead of fighting to grow, it fights to survive, with each blade drawing closer to the ground, trying to suck a last drop of water from the dry earth until the stalks lie tangled in defeat as the mower sits idly by.

The air is filled with an eerie quiet, as though you have suddenly found yourself immobile beneath a body of water and the sound is merely the pressure within your ears. Even the ice in the glass fails to betray the quiet, for it has barely remained intact on the short journey from the kitchen to the porch. The tea sits below a layer of melted ice with several remaining crystals fighting to stay afloat. The glass becomes covered with sweaty droplets, which cling tenaciously to the sides before slipping loose and sliding to rest on the side of the hand that holds it. On the hand, the water wells up and the drops regroup, sliding over each knuckle, pausing for a second, then dropping with the hope that they will hit the porch floor before they evaporate.

The silence is broken by the sound that comes like the ocean waves. It begins like a disturbed rattlesnake and, as it progresses, sounds like oiled kernels of popcorn shaking in the bottom of a tin pan. At its zenith, the sound is harsh, like a crude musical instrument made by a kindergartner who fills a Band-Aid box with dried black-eyed peas and then shakes with vigor. The sound is emitted from the cicada, the mothlike insect with a stout body, blunt head, and large transparent wings. Though you do not see them, there are hundreds in the yard around the porch all contributing to the raucous chorus. Their waves of sound are joined by the lilting Southern voice of Cordelia's mother. It hangs in the air as she tells Cordelia that she always calls them "protracted meeting bugs."

Cordelia asks her why, and she tells the story her mother told her on a similar afternoon with the cicada's songs filling the air. Cordelia is just a child, five or six, listening intently to her mother's story. She has disheveled hair, bare feet, and wide eyes. Her mother tells of a time of few cars and no cable television to bring preachers into your home. It was a time of traveling preachers who went from church to church across the rural South to hold protracted meetings. The preacher would stay at an isolated church for several days and families from an extended radius, some traveling all day, gathered for the event.

When the preacher came to the little church your grandmother went to, she tells Cordy, they would pile into a wagon with bedding, and food, everything they would need to stay at the church for several days. At the church, the preacher would preach and the congregation would sing while some would play guitar or banjo for accompaniment. Food would be laid out on long tables for a communal meal, and as the day ended, each family would sleep beneath their wagons. When Cordelia's grandmother lay under the wagon, she was unable to sleep because of the excitement and because the noises of the day continued to ring in her ears long after the church was silent. On the hot summer evenings, the ringing was replaced by the ebb and flow of an insect's lullaby that filled her head as she slept.

Her grandmother was told the insect was called a cicada, but she didn't listen, because the cicada and the protracted meetings were forever joined in her heart. The tradition continues in Cordelia's heart.

finally facing my Waterloo . . .

$\mathcal{W}$hat time is it? I never know what time it is. I don't suppose it matters, I don't have anywhere to go, but I hate waking up lost in time. The days are too short. It's always dark. I have always relished the darkness, but that was when I could see the clock. The truth is, I never really cared what time it was, or what day it was or even what year it was for that matter. Sasha gave me the best gift I ever received. For my birthday, she gave me a broken watch. My favorite book is *To Kill a Mockingbird*, and I was always quoting long passages from the book. Scout and Jem in the balcony of the courthouse, Miss Caroline from Winston County, and my favorite passage about Boo. People bring food with death and flowers with illness and little things in between. Boo was our neighbor. He brought us two soap dolls, a broken watch and chain, a pair of good-luck pennies and our lives. Sasha wrote the quote in a card in the box with the watch. It is a beautiful pocket watch with no case. The face is white with gold numbers and hands; all the wheels and gears are visible when you turn it over. It doesn't tick or tock or make any noise at all, and no matter when it is, it can be whatever time you want it to be. Any instant can be locked in time. The perfect gift for someone who never seemed to have anyplace to be but at her computer or reading.

Reading is a wonderful activity. You can do it any time or place and not have to have much equipment, only light. I have always read in a dim light. The optometrist said it didn't matter if I didn't strain my eyes. I never liked a harsh reading light; I like the low intimate light, just the two of us, me and my book.

I edited several best-sellers. A couple of great fiction collections. I liked fiction that was a bit quirky. I pushed a lot of writers no one else published. I rejected a lot of commercial authors. I read once in *io*, a funky little magazine from Austin, that the difference between writers and authors was their jacket photo. Authors looked like models; writers looked like they looked. I've been to enough readings to believe their assessment. Writers you recognize when they walk in, but authors bear no real resemblance to their jacket photo. Maybe I was never published because I had the wrong jacket photo. Matthew says that nowadays, you have to be famous or rich to get published. All the actors are doing it. First you need a movie; then you get a book published. Then, I guess, you sell the rights to the movies and star in your book.

Vice is nice, but incest is best.

*C*ordelia, how was the Queen? I ran into Delaney, said you had no English films."

"What time is it?"

"Five-thirty."

"Day or night?"

"They're both kinda day, aren't they?"

"Is this a quiz? This time of year they're both kinda night. It's dark. That's the kinda thing dying people always say. It's dark, but this time of year it is dark. But tell me, Doctor Campbell, is it five-thirty day or night?"

"It's late afternoon, Cordelia. I brought your mail."

"Didn't you bring it before?"

"Delaney must have picked it up this morning. It must have been yesterday's mail and this is today's mail."

"Catalogs?"

"A letter from the funeral home."

"Dying for my business."

"You're a card, Cordy. The doctor says I'm stable. No change."

"The doctor, your grandson?"

"You got a card with an obscene note."

"Great, I'll save it for later."

"They finally sold the Lawler house. Some doctor bought it."

"I thought it would go to a funeral home."

"Hell, we got three."

"One's enough."

"You're too young to know the Lawler sisters, aren't you?"

"They're dead."

"Been dead for quite some time."

"They had a dog funeral."

"Who told you about that? It was the damnedest thing, a big old funeral for that dog."

"They didn't have any kids, might as well send the dog out in style. Do you think dogs go to heaven?"

"I'm not convinced people go, Cordelia."

"A fine thing to tell a dying woman. Did you ever read Roald Dahl?"

"He was married to somebody."

"Patricia Neal. They're both dead. They had a kid die and one get hit in a stroller and she had a stroke. It was like the story of Job. After the kid died, Dahl was concerned about the afterlife. He said the process of dying can be undignified, but not death itself. He asked an archbishop if there was an afterlife. The guy says yes."

"He was an archbishop."

"Yeah, but Dahl is not convinced, so he says, 'What about dogs: do they qualify too?' 'Of course not,' he said, and Dahl said, 'I couldn't see it; if there was a God, didn't he make dogs too?' Maybe the Lawler sisters read a lot of Roald Dahl."

"Who knows."

$\mathcal{M}$argaret's gait was fit for a racehorse as she hurried to get to work at the cafe. With her husband off driving a truck somewhere up north, Margaret was left with the sole responsibility of their daughter, Taylor, a child Margaret had never really understood. This morning, after being scolded at five-minute intervals, Taylor locked herself in the bathroom and began screaming, "Please don't hit me again," while seated under the open window, causing Margaret untold embarrassment as she walked her daughter to the school bus stop.

Before Margaret reached the cafe, she saw one of the Lawler sisters cross the street to the side she was walking on. It was hard to tell the Lawler sisters apart unless they were standing side by side. Though they were not twins, their advanced years had left them similarly shriveled. As Margaret caught up with the old woman, she recognized Georgie Lawler, and saw that she was crying. Her immediate thought was that something had happened to Ruby Lawler, who was several years older than Georgie.

The two spinsters had been fixtures in Equality for as long as anyone could remember. Their father had wanted a house full of boys. He had tolerated the birth of one daughter, but was furious at the birth of a second and insisted upon calling her George, which led to a great deal of marital strain, and before long, the family existed in name only. When their mother's sister, Catherine Hunter Douglas, became infirm, Ruby came to stay with her, and Georgie soon followed. When their aunt died, they stayed on in the house, never marrying, though each had had numerous opportunities. That was over fifty years ago.

"Hello, Miss Lawler. Are you all right? Is your sister all right?"

"This has been the worst day of my life and it's not even eight o'clock." She sniffed through her tears.

"What's the matter? Is Ruby—"

"Sister had to be at the doctor early this morning and I was to go to the bank to sign some papers. We got a late start and things just fell apart. Sister left before breakfast and I was hurrying. I got ready to fix Buck's egg. I was late and he was already upset. When I cracked the egg the yolk broke and it was my last egg. Buck likes his eggs sunny-side up with no brown edges. I didn't have another egg, so I scrambled it for him." She caught her breath and sobbed more loudly. "He wouldn't eat it. I don't know what to do. He's going to be mad at me all day, and when Sister finds out, she's going to be mad, too."

Georgie was inconsolable as she and Margaret parted company in front of the Reed Funeral Home. The more Margaret thought of the old woman crying, the more she thought of that mangy Buck lying up on the sofa just waiting for Ruby to come in so that he could limp over on three legs while holding his crippled foot high and whimpering over an egg that was not cooked to his liking. He wouldn't be sitting up at the table eating eggs sunny-side up or otherwise if it hadn't been for Georgie Lawler; he'd just be a dead dog that no one remembered. Margaret wondered if maybe the Lawler sister would like to swap Taylor for Buck, just for a day.

Everyone remembered Buck. He was just a scroungy pup when he ventured on to the train tracks at the same time that the tracks were being changed for the arrival of the two-fifteen. His right rear paw landed between the rails at just the moment they were moved, causing Buck to find himself trapped. As pups will do, Buck howled a loud, despair-filled cry, and who should hear him but Georgie. She dropped the rake and ran to the tracks, grabbing the pup. When she realized he was trapped, she began howling with him, and soon everyone within earshot was crowded around the tracks.

"I'll put the little fellow out of his misery," volunteered a police office, but Georgie threw her body over the dog. By the time the mayor and the police chief arrived, the train could be heard in the distance.

"Talk to her, Ruby," the mayor pleaded. "You have got to get her off the track, the train is coming."

"I can't do it, Mr. Mayor. Sister has made up her mind. She's not leaving the dog."

"What'll I do, Ruby?"

"You'll have to stop the train."

She looked at the mayor and he looked at her and neither flinched. Ruby patted her sister's head as she looked at the mayor.

"There, there, Sister. Everything is all right. The mayor will stop the train."

The mayor grabbed the police chief and they huddled for a second. Dickie Reed slapped the mayor's back.

"I'll give them a package deal," he said as the police chief caught the mayor's arm.

"I'll just be damned if I watch two old ladies and a dog get mangled by a train not a block from Main Street." He grabbed the chief. "Stop that train."

"How?"

"Send somebody up the track with a flag. Wave it down. I don't know how, but stop it."

A deputy was looking for something to wave, when someone in the crowd offered the chief a Confederate flag. The mayor yelled out as the train whistle grew nearer, and the chief and deputy ran up the tracks. Several youngsters decided to follow, and so did the owner of the flag. Soon, about twenty people were running up the tracks toward the train to save Georgie and the dog.

The train was traveling mighty slowly as it rounded the curve into Equality. It came to a stop as the engineer shook his head at the sight of an overweight police chief waving a rebel flag, followed by two dozen schoolchildren, the auto mechanic, a mailman, half the Baptist Bible class, and the town drunk.

"You all trying to secede again?" he asked as he climbed down from the cab. As he walked up the tracks toward the sisters, he found himself surrounded by a cheering mob.

"I haven't seen this big a crowd since the FDR funeral train," he said.

Ruby Lawler introduced herself and her sister, explaining the problem. The engineer tipped his hat.

"I'm Bernard Rogers, but my friends call me Buck."

After surveying the situation, Mr. Rogers manually switched the track, freeing the dog. Georgie was so pleased she decided at that moment to name the dog after the engineer.

Everyone still tells the story, though the details often change. Margaret remembered that Taylor was telling her the story several months ago. Taylor's version had the wheels of the train ripping the hem of Georgie's skirt, and Buck Rogers jumping off the train and bending the tracks with his bare hands to free the dog and Georgie. Then, according to Taylor, he asked Miss Lawler to marry him, but she couldn't leave her sister. Margaret wanted to tell Taylor that Buck Rogers's real name was Bernard. She also wanted her to know that Georgie Lawler was seventy-two years old when she saved the dog, and no matter what Taylor had heard, Bernard and Georgie were not a likely couple. However, Margaret did not like to argue with Taylor, so she let her version of the story stand.

Three days after seeing Georgie crying on the street, Margaret was informed of the tragic news that Buck had passed away. As it turned out, Buck's failure to eat the scrambled eggs had less to do with the way in which they were prepared, and more to do with the fact that after fifteen years of high living, Buck was ready to meet his maker.

At the cafe, Buck's sad death was big news. Those who were closest to the family said as the end grew near, Georgie called Dr. Campbell, who tried to explain that he knew nothing about treating dogs. The sisters were in such distress, however, that the doctor paid an unusual house call. Shortly after his arrival, Buck died.

Ruby and Georgie threw themselves into the funeral plans. Dr. Campbell was asked to call the Reed Funeral Home to ask Dickie Reed to come and get Buck. The sisters wanted him embalmed. After his initial laughter, Dickie shouted to the doctor, "I'll be damned if I'll embalm a dog."

Ruby Lawler removed her phone from the doctor's hand, calmly telling Dickie there was a fifty-dollar bonus for the job. Within minutes, Dickie had come for Buck's body.

The sisters paid a visit to the casket factory and special-ordered a casket befitting Buck. It was lined with a light blue crushed velvet, so that Buck's white fur and dark brown patches would show up. There was to be a large funeral and wake for Buck. A state senator had already agreed to deliver a eulogy. Everyone in town was set to go to the funeral. Even the cafe was closing. At the railroad tracks, where Buck had his initial brush with death, children were placing flowers. Some were zinnias and geraniums from their mothers' yards, while others laid dandelions and Queen Anne's lace gathered from the roadside.

Buck was laid to rest with all the pomp and circumstance of a reigning head of state. He was interred under his favorite tree in the garden. The funeral was written up in the Birmingham paper, but Taylor was forced to hear the details secondhand. Margaret walked Taylor to the railroad tracks to lay the marigolds that she had ripped up by the roots from the flower box. It was the proper send-off for Buck, she told the little girl. "You're too young for funerals. Even dog funerals. Besides, you don't have anything to wear."

I'm going to wear black to my funeral. This is not a big surprise to anyone who knows me. Most of my wardrobe is black. Some editor at *Vogue* decided a while back that black was out. She was no longer going to wear black and no one else who was to be in vogue should wear it either. This lasted until she needed to travel to Europe and had to be on a plane for a long time. Suddenly, she realized how important black was to the female wardrobe.

I am wearing a nice black wool suit. With slacks, not a skirt. Just because I'm going to be dead doesn't mean I'm going to be uncomfortable. I have always preferred funerals to weddings. I think it's because of the dark clothes. At funerals, everyone is on their best behavior, and they are dressed in black. Everyone looks better in black, even children. My mother dressed me in black as a child, long before it was a popular idea. My favorite picture from my childhood is of me in a black cashmere sweater and pearls. My blond hair is pulled back with a black hairband and I have a stupid, forced smirk. I haven't changed much. I will look about the same in the casket. Black sweater, blond hair pulled back with a black headband, pearls, and a smirk. My eyes will be closed and I'll be almost forty years older, but little will have changed.

allons danser . . .

> Dear Cordelia
> What the fuck is happening? Come back. Please come back. You can have all the Black Sparrow Bowles. Don't leave me.
>
> Matthew

*M*atthew calls her twice a week. Sometimes she is coherent and they talk and laugh as though nothing has changed. Sometimes she doesn't quite remember who he is. Matthew would have come down to stay with her to the end, but she made him promise not to come. They had their good-byes and that was the end for Cordelia. Matthew won't let go. He keeps the postcards coming, hoping she might give in and see him, but Cordelia is tough. Sasha is another story. She understands how Cordelia feels and won't push her. She writes and calls and sends little gifts, pretending Cordelia is not going to die, but knowing that the end is near. Sasha would keep her appointment with the hairdresser the morning of Armageddon. Perhaps it was her attention to order that kept her from Cordelia. She had been a lousy lover but she was a great friend.

Cordelia once said she wanted to be a Spanish dancer. Sasha said you should follow your dreams, so she booked lessons with a flamenco dancer. Sasha slicked her hair back, donned toreador pants and a short jacket, and showed up with a single red rose. Cordy pulled her blond hair back in a tight bun, popped open a fan, and the dancing began. They made a dashing couple as long as they didn't dance. For the first time ever, the flamenco dancer was tempted to refund the money for the lessons. With each lesson Sasha's rose grew more wilted, and the harder they tried, the more comical they became. In the end, Cordelia realized that she was not cut out to be a Spanish dancer, but she had given it a try, and now there would never be any doubt in her mind. She no longer wanted to be a Spanish dancer; there were other dreams ahead.

Cordy,

Saw this card and thought it would remind you of me. Actually, my hips were never this narrow and I never owned the lace underwear. But I do have the jeans and the jacket. That counts for something.

Sasha

$\mathcal{T}$he title of the picture on the postcard is "Cheeky Lace." A woman in a leather jacket is pulling on her jeans. Perhaps she is taking them off. For years historians have debated whether the central panel in the Sistine Chapel depicts the fingers of God and Adam pulling apart or getting ready to touch. The debate goes on. In the postcard, the woman's fingers are hooked into the waistband of the jeans. Her hip is cocked to one side and she is wearing a pair of high-cut, lace panties. I think she is pulling on her jeans, but I hope she is taking them off.

Doctor Campbell tells me my lungs are like lace. I look closely at the fine black lace covering her hips. I wonder if my lungs are as beautiful as the lace on her hips.

Mr. Delaney brought in the card. He didn't read the note but noticed the handwriting. He thinks Sasha is a man. Why would a woman send another woman a "Cheeky Lace" card? That Sasha has pretty handwriting for a boy, he says.

not much between despair and ecstasy . . .

$\mathcal{B}$rought your lunch. How are you today?"

"What time is it?"

"It's eleven-thirty in the morning, Cordelia."

"What day is it?"

"Tuesday."

"Who are you?"

"Mr. Delaney, from the church. I bring your food every day. Every day but Sunday."

"The Methodist Church?"

"That's the one."

"On Main Street?"

"Yep."

"My family went to that church."

"Every last one of them."

"That would be me. Do you know Mother's cousin Augusta?"

"I did know her."

"She went to prison."

"Augusta?"

"The women's prison."

"Augusta was in Julia Tutwiler?"

"She went to sing."

*T*he Tutwiler family was a prestigious Alabama family. Many things were named after them. Augusta thought immediately of the Tutwiler Hotel in Birmingham, the place where most newlyweds in Equality had spent their honeymoons. There were libraries and banks with the Tutwiler name, and Augusta was sure there had been a governor or a senator who was a Tutwiler, and probably a general in the Confederate Army. But she couldn't figure out why a prison was named after a Tutwiler, especially Miss Julia.

After considerable reflection, Augusta became convinced she had stumbled upon the answer to her question. Actually, she had three possible answers to why the prison was named after Julia Tutwiler. The first possibility, thought Augusta, was that there had been a list of things to name after Tutwilers and a list of Tutwilers to name them after, and both Miss Julia and the prison were at the bottom of their lists, but this was too logical. Next came the notion that since Miss Julia was a woman, they wanted to name a women's building after her. Since the Teacher's College for Women at Montgomery already had a name, the only thing left was the women's prison. Augusta felt this was plausible. Her favorite explanation, however, was that Miss Julia Tutwiler had been a rounder in her day and the family felt naming a prison after her was a fitting and proper tribute.

The children's choir from the Methodist church had been asked to sing at the Julia Tutwiler Prison for Women just outside Montgomery. The warden wanted to provide a bit of culture for the women at the facility, and Mr. Harris, the new preacher, had obliged, citing Christian duty to those less fortunate. At nine o'clock on a September Saturday morning, a rickety school bus pulled up in front of the Methodist Church, its engine continuing to run a few minutes after the ignition had been turned off. The outside of the bus was a warm orange color, like the pumpkins that were beginning to appear in the gardens of Equality. The inside of the bus resembled an army footlocker, with the dark green interior smelling of unlaundered clothing. Fifteen members of the children's choir, the preacher, and the music director boarded the school bus bound for the prison.

Augusta sat three rows from the last seat. She looked out of the window as the bus rambled down the road. Most of what she saw was a blur because she spent her time trying to stay on her seat as the bus lurched and bucked over the country roads. Augusta was wearing the same dress she had worn to her mother's funeral three years earlier. She had not grown much since she was seven, with the exception of the four inches that had done nothing but make her skinny legs longer. Her aunt Cordelia had added a ruffle to the bottom so that Augusta could still wear the calico dress.

Augusta soon lost interest in the scenery and gained a familiarity with the jerky movements of the bus. She began to think about the Julia Tutwiler Prison for Women. She had never been to a prison before and had never thought that a woman could do anything to end up in prison. Since she had no conception of the women in the prison, she began to think about Julia Tutwiler.

As the bus turned off the main road, the driver proceeded down a short stretch of red clay and gravel and pulled up to a tall chain-link fence, next to which stood a small house for the guards. A large man in a gray uniform checked his clipboard and waved the bus onto the prison grounds. From the bus windows, the prison looked like a big gray box. The bus driver parked at the small door where a man waited. He boarded the bus and spoke with Reverend Harris for a few minutes. He was a slight man who wore tiny round glasses with gold rims that pinched his nose. "So glad you could come," he said, and he ushered the choir off the bus and through the door.

The door itself was the same size as the front door of a house, but it led to a large, sparsely furnished room, painted the same gray as the outside of the prison. At the back of the room there was a large gate made out of long steel bars that stretched from the floor to the ceiling. Beside the gate was a small wooden desk, and at the desk sat a guard in a uniform that reminded Augusta of a police uniform, but which lacked the bright navy color. The choir lined up behind the preacher, the warden, and the music director like chicks in a row and marched through the gates that the man in the gray police uniform opened.

They walked down a long corridor where even the slightest sound echoed, which made it easy for the preacher to pick out anyone who was not on his best behavior. Soon they approached another steel gate where a guard counted and checked and waved the choir through. Augusta noticed that the doors on either side of this hallway had signs with official-sounding titles, and when they passed the door with the word "Warden," the man with the wire-rimmed glasses said to Mr. Harris, "That's mine." They reached a third set of gates and Augusta suddenly found she was breathing faster, and she could hear her heart pounding. She remembered the last time she felt like this.

She had been fishing at her uncle's lake when her brother Thaddeus teased her about not wanting to go in for a swim.

"Augusta's a baby," Thaddeus said.

"Am not," Augusta answered.

"Augusta can't swim because she's a baby."

"Don't want to swim."

"Can't swim."

"Everyone can swim," their uncle said. "It's a God-given talent, like breathing." With those words he lifted Augusta up from the dock and pitched her into the dark water of the lake. Augusta sank. The water surrounded her, holding her in the darkness. She struggled to the surface to yell for help, and took in a mouthful of water. She sank again as the water distorted the sounds of her own heart beating. The action was repeated only once before Thaddeus jumped in and pulled her to the shore. As she cried and coughed, she heard her uncle say, "You didn't leave her in there long enough. She would have gotten herself out." But Augusta knew that she couldn't have fought the water.

She thought about being trapped under the water with no way of escaping. That was how she felt now. As the last gate slammed closed behind her, she felt she was again sinking in the lake. The choir entered the recreation room, which was large and square, with only a little light filtering in from the barred windows high overhead. There was a tiny wooden stage erected for the choir that raised them only a foot off the gray cement floor. There were a few women milling about and Augusta tried not to stare, although she desperately wanted to see what convicts, especially women convicts, looked like. The first thing Augusta noticed was their dresses, all identical gray smocks with the exception of the numbers on the front.

The room was damp and musty and smelled gray, Augusta thought. She closed her eyes tightly and tried to imagine a new box of crayons and what they looked like when you first open them. She tried to see in her mind the raw umber and turquoise and rose, and she tried to remember the difference between yellow-orange and orange-yellow. She was afraid in all the gray that she could no longer remember colors, and she wondered if the women in the prison ever imagined new crayons.

As the children waited to mount the platform to sing, Augusta overheard the warden talking to the preacher. She picked up only bits and pieces. Most of the women were from big cities, Montgomery or Mobile. Most had helped their men commit crimes. The warden's voice got louder as Augusta listened. "There is one from your parts," he said to the preacher. "Came to us about four years ago." The preacher hadn't been there four years and he looked puzzled. "She had three babies, oldest one was three. The husband ran out on her. One day she took the kids to the bridge over Hatchet Creek. Dropped them in one by one. Watched them sink. The police, doctors, everyone asked her why. Only reason she ever gave . . . all she ever said was, 'Because it was Saturday.' Can you imagine? That's her, high-strung girl, the one with the long blond hair."

Augusta looked out at almost twenty gray women, and sitting somewhat removed from the group was a slender woman with long hair. Augusta wasn't sure what "high-strung" meant, but there was something different about the woman who had thrown her kids into Hatchet Creek. She had no time to figure it out then, because the music director told them to get up on the platform and get ready to sing.

An old upright piano, badly in need of tuning, provided background for the singers, and they followed the piano's lead, singing off-key. They sang everyone's favorites, "Blessed Assurance," "Jesus Loves Me," "Onward Christian Soldiers." Augusta forgot the words to "Onward Christian Soldiers" because she was so distracted by the story of the woman with the long hair. She watched her throughout the recital, and as the singing ended, she remembered where she had seen a face with that kind of look.

Augusta and Thaddeus had spent the summer at their aunt Cordelia's. There was a fat, brown, striped mama cat who had had a litter of kittens in the woods. As the kittens got older, the mama cat led them to Cordelia's for food. Augusta watched every day, and her summer project became the taming of the kittens. She managed to capture several of them over the next few days and they were becoming used to her touch. One particular kitten always managed to avoid being caught.

Everything went fine until the day a friendly but large dog entered Cordelia's yard at kitten feeding time. Kittens scattered everywhere, climbing trees, ducking under logs and scurrying to the woods. Augusta and Thaddeus forced the dog to leave, but the kittens remained hidden. Augusta scouted the yard and found only one kitten. The bright yellow ball of fur that had always gotten away was down in the gutter by the basement window. Augusta lay on her stomach, talking to the frightened cat who backed away from her. She reached out, grabbing for the kitten whose mouth opened, uttering a combination hiss-growl, and its tiny paw struck out at Augusta's face. Rolling over and sitting up, she saw a yellow blur like a streak of sunlight head into the woods.

When the choir stepped off the platform, several of the prisoners spoke to the children and the preacher. Augusta could not take her eyes off the woman who never moved from the gray folding chair. Augusta moved closer. Neither of them spoke. The woman's eyes focused and she slowly raised her hand, stopping for a second before reaching out and touching her hand to Augusta's cheek. Augusta took her hand. A rough jerk from the preacher separated them.

"Get back into line, Augusta." Reverend Harris's voice was distant. The choir marched out in single file with Augusta looking back over her shoulder at the strange woman. Retracing their same steps, the choir began to leave the prison. Augusta could see the door at the end of the big room they had entered, and her breathing relaxed as she saw the rays of light shining through the window.

The first set of gates opened, and the choir filed through. As Augusta passed in front of the guard, he reached out with his giant hand and pulled her back. His voice rang out. "You got too many, Preacher. This one will have to stay." He held her for just a second, then pushed her through the gates toward the choir and closed them as he laughed. The warden didn't laugh at his employee's joke. Augusta was sure that, as frightened as she was, she couldn't have looked as scared as the warden. His face was green, Augusta thought, sea green, as she stepped out the door into the sunlight.

FATHER KILLS CHILDREN, SELF
IN NORTH CAROLINA

KILL DEVIL HILLS, N.C.——Residents left flowers and notes on the blackened spot of pavement where the bodies of three murdered children were found in a burning van. Their father committed suicide nearby.

Even Police Chief James Grady, a 20-year law enforcement veteran who also served with Special Forces in Vietnam, was shaken by what he saw this weekend. "It's an American story. It bothers all of our consciences because somewhere, someplace, society has failed to prevent this kind of thing from happening."

The children's mother, who had been separated from her husband since October, had reported them missing from their home in Delaware after they did not return from visiting their father. Police identified the children as Susan Denise Franklin, 9; Robert James Brown, 6; and Christina Marie Brown, 4.

The children died of gunshot wounds to the head before the fire, said a spokesman for Pitt Memorial Hospital in Greenville, where the autopsies were performed.

On Monday morning, a green basket of silk flowers had been left at the scene of the fire with a sign saying "To the three little angels." The van and the bodies had been removed.

I miss Sasha. I miss her body, generous and warm. We were lovers for about a week but realized it wouldn't work. I didn't care that much about the sex, but I loved her body, it was comforting and friendly. We talked for hours about the failure of the language to describe the relationships of women adequately. I would say men are good for two things, one of which is heavy lifting. Sasha thought the only thing men were good for was heavy lifting, and she was sure with a little time, she could find a woman to lift anything. Sasha was cavalierly sapphic; her body was her own and she would use it as she pleased. I loved the way she loved her body. Sasha was not off-the-rack skin; she lived in her body and wore her skin like it had been designed for her by Balenciaga.

I loved to sleep with Sasha, long after the sex was gone; she would let me into her bed and hold me. I've thought about what women want in their lives. Most of them want intimacy, not sex. They want someone to talk to, but too often they pay a therapist $75 a week just to have someone to talk to. Sasha talked to me and we would spend our $75 on extravagant lunches, then go back to her apartment and fall into bed. I would wrap my arms around her and sleep. Where does another woman find a Sasha? Women are taught to be leery of each other. Other women want your man, daughters want their father's affection, girlfriends would dump you on a Saturday night for a date; if they don't want your man, then perhaps they want you! It's no wonder that women don't get along. Programmed into off-the-rack skin, caught in a language they did not invent, forced into a culture of black and white, where is their humanity, their sexuality? Where are their souls?

Cordelia."

"Sasha?"

"No, it's Gabrielle. How are you feeling?"

"Not too good now that you and your needles are here."

"Just want you to feel better."

"The capital of Somalia is Mogadishu."

"Very good. But why don't you wait till the shot."

"Gabrielle, do you believe in God?"

"Yes, I do."

"Why?"

"Why not."

"I suppose that's a good answer in my condition. There's not much sin left in me, so you might as well believe."

"So you believe in God."

"I believe. I've always believed, but I don't think God is some old white man."

"Some old white woman?"

"Not exactly."

"What do you think God looks like?"

"I think God looks like Jill Clayburgh."

"The actress."

"Yeah. Like she looked in *An Unfinished Woman*. There was always something about the way she looked then. Will Rogers said, 'God created man in his own image and man returned the compliment.' The Bible says we are all created in the image of God, so it makes sense that I would think God was a blond, white woman."

"You might be right. And what about heaven?"

"I think heaven is a lot like Hilton Head. On my island there are many condos; if it wasn't so I would have told you."

"What, no pearly gates?"

"Most scholars believe that people endow heaven with the particular riches of the age. In Biblical times, heaven had pearly gates and streets paved with gold. Now the most valuable thing you can have is beachfront property, so heaven would look like Hilton Head. Besides, I'm a Southerner; heaven has to be warm. I can't imagine heaven being like Stowe. I'd be miserable. I'd just wander around cold and cranky, thinking to myself that I should have gone to hell. At least it would be warm and friends would be there."

"Dr. Campbell's right about you, Cordy, you're a card. So, when you get to Hilton Head Heaven, who's the first person you want to see?"

"Janis Joplin."

"You're going to heaven and you want to see Janis Joplin. What about Jesus?"

"The line is probably too long, like trying to see Santa Claus in Macy's at Christmas. Everybody will want to say hello to Jesus and tell their crucifixion stories. I just want to find Janis and ask her if Dick Cavett was good in bed."

"Dick Cavett. Are you serious?"

"I'll tell the details if I can get out of this shot?"

"No."

"Then ask me only capitals of warm countries. Is Somalia warm?"

"I believe it is. Now what is the capital of the Bahamas?"

"Nassau."

"What's the capital of Guatemala?"

"Guatemala?"

"That's right."

"What?"

"Guatemala is the capital of Guatemala. Try Panama."

"Panama City."

"No. That's the capital of Florida. It's just Panama. Okay, how about Mexico?"

"Mexico City."

"Very good!"

"Do you believe in God?"

"Yes. Do you?"

"In God, but not in preachers."

There were those people in Equality who would offer the opinion that Peter Paul Sullivan was the devil incarnate. Mr. Joe Carter did not believe in gods or devils, but he knew that his wife did. That's why he would often tell her that one day he was going to hold the boy down and shave his head and show her the mark of the beast that was surely tattooed on his scalp. After twenty-five years of marriage, Adelaide Carter still cringed when her

husband's language bordered on the blasphemous. She told him on many occasions that a child who had no mother and was raised by a religious zealot was bound to be a bit rambunctious.

The Preacher Sullivan had come to Alabama from Tennessee and had begun his ministry from the tiny Pentecostal church that sat on a large, weedy lot on the same side of main street as the Shiloh Baptist church. The First United Methodist church was on the opposite side of the street, and when the sun shone a certain way, the shadow of the Methodist bell tower lay on the ground in front of the Pentecostal church. It had been several years since the church had had a preacher. The last one had been a skittish boy who had often stepped into the pulpit and forgotten his sermon, leaving the congregation to sing to itself. There was little time for singing with the Preacher Sullivan in the pulpit. He preached Wednesdays and Sundays, and once every other month he led the congregation to Hatchet Creek and baptized the newly converted in the slow, stagnant water. Rumor soon spread through Equality that his faith was so strong that he could reach down and grasp a serpent without fear; he could speak in tongues, make the blind see, the deaf hear, and the lame walk.

"If you ask me," said Joe Carter, "the Preacher Sullivan is the lame one."

"Joe, don't you talk like that," said Mrs. Carter.

"If there's anything Equality don't need, it's Holy Roller snake charmers."

"Joe!"

"If you ask me, the Preacher Sullivan was born too late. I don't know if he can handle snakes, but he would have made a great snake oil salesman."

"No one asked you, Joe."

"If you ask me, the snake he ought to be handling is that boy of his. Peter Paul Sullivan is as mean as a water moccasin in heat."

"Joe Carter! God will strike you dead."

"Whose God? His or yours? They can duke it out for me."

On the last Sunday in July, long after the Baptists and the Methodists were finished with Sunday dinner, the Pentecostal church was still in session. Peter Paul sat in his usual spot, the first row pew, right in front of the pulpit that held his father. The boy could sit for hours watching his father, as though the preacher were a magician.

The Preacher Sullivan stepped out of the pulpit and moved in front of the altar below the cross. He stood before the congregation. His arms were outstretched, a Bible lay in his right hand, and a black robe covered his body, making him look as though he were the shadow cast by the cross. He had visited a sick woman, he told his followers. She had a cancer, but God was calling her forward to save her. The congregation became restless, shifting in their seats and fanning furiously as they looked for the woman called by God.

Mrs. Jenkins headed for the altar, tears rolling down her cheeks. Her body, heavy and covered with sweat, moved steadily, like a plow horse. The Preacher Sullivan had spent most of Thursday with Mrs. Jenkins. She had told him she was sure she had cancer, even though the doctor had found nothing but a touchy gallbladder. She asked the preacher to pray for her, and later she fixed his supper. Everything but the cake had been fried, and the Preacher Sullivan noticed that the warmth of the kitchen mixed with the greasy steam made the air feel as slick as boiled okra.

The Preacher Sullivan told Mrs. Jenkins of his distrust of doctors. The only true healing came from God, he told her. He was worried that she was going to get sick, and the doctors couldn't do a thing because they wouldn't believe. He made her promise that if she got sick, she would come to his Sunday service, and he would cast out her demons.

The congregation's attention was fixed on the events at the altar. Peter Paul watched as his father took Mrs. Jenkins's hands. All the fans were still, and the church felt like moldy bread in a damp plastic bag. The murmurs of prayers and the amens were suddenly drowned out by the shouts of the Preacher Sullivan.

He opened his mouth and unknown utterances poured forth as though he were the announcer on a foreign language radio station with poor reception. Peter Paul had heard his father speak in tongues on several occasions, and he did not know how or why it happened, only that the occurrence was very important.

The preacher raised his hand to the heavens and then drove the heel of his hand into the forehead of Mrs. Jenkins. As he screamed for her to be healed, the hand and forehead made contact, sounding like the explosion of a single damp firecracker. Mrs. Jenkins fell to the floor amid the shouts of hallelujah.

The church was now quiet. Peter Paul held his father's Bible as though it were the Holy Grail. His eyes were fixed on his father. He was proud that the preacher could heal the sick just like Jesus. He had watched him heal hundreds of people. He remembered one man in Tennessee whom his father had healed several times in various churches on the circuit he preached. The Preacher Sullivan was busy counting the day's offerings. He knew that healings were better than baptisms to fill the collection plate.

The Preacher Sullivan turned his lanky body toward Peter Paul and tousled the boy's sweaty blond hair. It was the first time that Sunday that the father had paid attention to his son. They had led a vagabond life since Peter Paul's mother had left them seven years earlier. She had not cared for the humdrum life of a small-town preacher's wife, and she headed for Memphis with a traveling salesman.

The Preacher Sullivan remained optimistic after his wife's departure, and he was always telling Peter Paul that one day they would find their land of milk and honey. There they would build a church—not just a church, but a cathedral. People would travel for days to see the cathedral and to hear the Preacher Sullivan's sermons. When Peter Paul grew older, he could preach beside his father in the cathedral. They would probably be on the television every Sunday, and they would receive thousands of contributions from the people they saved. They would have a large house and someone to cook dinner for them. That was in the future. The Preacher Sullivan took Peter Paul's hand and led him home to an empty house to fix Sunday dinner.

Mondays were always slow in the hardware store. Mr. Carter opened the store a half hour later on the first day of the work week to give himself some extra weekend time. Even though the faded red sign that had hung in the door of the Carter's hardware store for twenty years said that the store opened on Monday at ten o'clock, anyone in Equality could tell you that Mr. Joe Carter would not be in until ten-thirty.

Mr. Carter had seen only three customers in the store by the time Mrs. Carter arrived at midday.

"Here's your lunch, Joe," said Mrs. Carter.

"Thank you, dear. I saw some cars at the Holy Roller church this morning. Do you think he kept them overnight? You better hope that preacher of yours don't try to compete with the Preacher Sullivan, or I'll have to find someone else to fix my Sunday dinner."

"Joe! They are not Holy Rollers. I admit they do hold long services on Sunday but—"

"I wish he'd hold services every day so that boy of his would stay out of this store."

"Joe, the boy comes here because he likes you."

"Dear God, I'm going to have to go back to church so that you'll call off the little devil."

"Joe, please don't talk like that. Now go into your office and eat your lunch, I'll watch the store."

"Watch for my dear friend Peter Paul. That boy always walks out of here with something, and one day I'm going to catch him in the act."

Mr. Carter went to his office and Mrs. Carter began to straighten the seed packages in the rack. The bell over the door rang and in walked Peter Paul Sullivan, who began to browse. In Tennessee, Peter Paul had become a talented shoplifter, and he had transplanted this skill to Alabama. He loved the challenge of the illegal game, and he found that Mr. Carter offered the most sport.

Peter Paul stood in front of the fishing tackle. Before him lay a vast array of tempting objects. There were silver sinkers in assorted sizes, gold hooks with sharp barbs, and dozens of sticky plastic worms in enough colors to fill a kaleidoscope. Mr. Carter watched the boy; the sound of the bell and the lack of adult voices had made him get up from his lunch and look into the store. He quietly slipped up behind Peter Paul and grabbed him, lifting the boy's feet slightly off the ground and causing him to shake like the rubber worm he held in his hand.

"I've got you now, you little thief."

"Joe, what's the problem?" said Mrs. Carter.

"I caught him trying to steal tackle. What do you have to say, boy?"

"Now, Joe, don't upset the child."

"The devil's got a hold of you, Mr. Carter," Peter Paul said. "My dad says the devil can make you do strange things."

"Your dad is the one who does strange things, boy."

"Don't talk about my dad. God talks to my dad, and he heals people like Jesus did."

"Your dad couldn't make a dog heel."

"Joe! Just let him go."

"You better talk to him, Mrs. Carter. One day he may get sick and need my daddy to heal him, but God won't let it happen, 'cause he don't believe. You got to believe, Mr. Carter."

"I believe that if you set foot in here again, I'll turn you across my knee and teach you a lesson."

"Let him go, Joe!"

"Get out, Peter Paul, and don't you come back."

"Repent now, Mr. Carter. Good day, ma'am." The boy bowed slightly as he left.

"He's basically a good boy, Joe. He just needs someone to look after him."

"He needs a swift kick."

Mrs. Carter stayed in the store most of the afternoon, arranging seeds and waiting on customers. Right before the store closed, she headed home to fix Joe's dinner. She passed by the Shiloh Baptist church and continued up the street. Out by the old cemetery, a group of children had gathered. They seemed unusually preoccupied, but Mrs. Carter was too busy thinking about dinner to pay attention to the children's games.

Becky Thomas was a frail and high-strung child who could begin sobbing or faint with only the slightest provocation. She sat at the edge of the cemetery beside a crumbling gravestone, crying and cradling a small box. Peter Paul had his arm around her shoulder, offering comfort. In the box lay Miss Kitty, Becky's young calico cat. Miss Kitty had misjudged the speed of an oncoming car and had paid for the mistake with her life.

Peter Paul suggested that they conduct a funeral for Miss Kitty. Burial could take place on the church lot. Becky's grief was momentarily assuaged. Carrying the shoe box that had been transformed into a cat coffin, Peter Paul led the children to the Pentecostal church lot. As he brandished a shovel from underneath the church steps, Peter Paul instructed one of the boys to dig the grave. He told one of the girls to gather some flowers from the lot which was filled with dandelions and Queen Anne's lace. Peter Paul went into the church and returned with a Bible in his hand. Assembling the multitude, the boy began to preach.

"In my house there are many rooms. I wouldn't have told you this if I didn't mean it." Peter Paul's voice rose in the summer air. "For God so loved the little animals that he had Noah build an ark to save them from the flood. God loves Miss Kitty, Becky, and he's going to look after her."

As Peter Paul and another boy lowered the cardboard casket into the ground, the Westminster chimes at the Methodist church began to play. They played as the burial continued, and as the flowers were placed on top of the grave, the bells struck six. The children dispersed. Sometime around nine-thirty, after darkness had fallen on Equality, Peter Paul returned to Miss Kitty's grave. He removed the flowers, already wilted in the heat, and unearthed the shoe box. He reached inside and lifted out the cat, placing it on the ground beside him. Reburying the box and returning the limp plants, he grabbed the cat's tail and headed toward Mr. Carter's store, swinging the carcass as he walked.

Behind the store, there was a small opening covered with screen near the ground. It allowed access to the shallow crawl space under the store. Peter Paul removed a hammer from the loop on his overalls and pried off the screen. He slid into the crawl space, dragging the carcass with him.

The boy knew that Mr. Carter's office was at the back of the store, so he moved on his back to that place directly under the office. Mr. Carter left the lamp on for protection, and fine rays of light filtered through the cracks in the floor, providing ample illumination. Above his head was a wooden floor joist.

Peter Paul took some ten-penny nails from his pocket. He lifted the carcass, and held it in place with his forearm, and began to nail the cat's body to the joist. When the cat was securely in place, he crawled out, replaced the screen, and walked home. It was several days before the full impact of Peter Paul's deed became evident. The hot, humid weather took its toll, and Joe Carter could no longer eat his lunch in his office.

"I checked the screen. I don't see how anything could have gotten under there," said Mr. Carter.

"Well, something did, Joe," said Mrs. Carter. "Maybe it dug its way in. Why don't you go and look?"

"I'll let you climb under and look for bodies."

"Sorry, Joe. Let's lock up, and we'll go home for lunch."

"Okay." As Joe locked the door, a familiar voice greeted him.

"Hi, Mr. Carter, nice weather today." Peter Paul smiled as he walked toward the church.

The August sun burned down on Equality, and several weeks went by before Mr. Carter's office grew inhabitable. The grass on the lot of the Pentecostal church had grown high, and the Preacher Sullivan had instructed Peter Paul to mow the weed-filled lawn. As the boy pushed the lawnmower to the church, its squeaky left front tire made a high-pitched sound, causing his jaw to ache, as though he were biting into a lemon. He left the mower at the church and walked to the Gulf station to fill the gas can.

When he returned to the lot, Peter Paul cranked up the mower and began his chore. Within an hour, both the boy and the mower were hot, empty, and covered with grass. Peter Paul turned on the spigot at the side of the church, letting it run until the water lost its rusty color, and then he took a drink. He carried the gas can to the mower and removed the hot tank cover, ignoring the warning information.

He began to pour the gasoline into the tank. A clap of distant thunder momentarily distracted him and the flammable liquid accidentally splashed onto the heated motor, causing it to ignite. The fire raced up the stream of gasoline and into the can, causing it to explode in Peter Paul's hands. The child was enveloped in flames.

The ambulance took the boy to the hospital in Alexander City. His father arrived shortly after the ambulance. The prognosis was grim; there was nothing the doctor could do. He would try to keep the child free from pain until the end, not an easy feat since there was little skin left to hold in the painkillers.

The Preacher Sullivan entered his son's room. The lights were dim. The sheet was suspended above the body like the drape in a magic act. As he bent over to look at his son, his knees buckled and his body hit the floor. He came to in a chair by the hospital bed.

Peter Paul called out to his father. The Preacher Sullivan drew closer to his son to comfort him. The boy's voice was strained and raspy as he spoke to his father. Peter Paul had a single request. "Heal me, Daddy," he said. The Preacher Sullivan sat back in the chair, buried his head in his hands, and wept.

While the night dragged on, the Preacher Sullivan sat helplessly watching his son die as the two words hung in the air around his head. "Heal me."

It had been two months since the accident. The oppressive heat of summer had given way to the cool brisk air of autumn, its red evening skies casting a pink haze on Equality. Main Street came to life each day at three as the children made their way home from school.

The side door of the Pentecostal church banged in the October breeze. The Preacher Sullivan had taken Peter Paul's body back to Tennessee and had never returned. Without a preacher, the congregation had found other places to worship. Vandals had broken into the tiny church, tearing the lock from the door and breaking windows, but they found nothing of value.

Mr. Carter removed the screen at the back of the hardware store and crawled under the building. With winter coming on, it was time to wrap the pipes under the store so that they wouldn't freeze and burst during Equality's brief cold spell. His flashlight shone on an object that startled him and caused him to jerk and hit his head. He flashed the light on the object again. Before him were the remains of a small animal, bits of fur and bones, held in place by ten-penny nails.

"The little son of a—" Mr. Carter caught his words midsentence, for even he could not speak ill of the dead. He found the pipes and wrapped them tightly, stopping on more than one occasion to shake his head and laugh.

"Guess what I found under the store?"

"What?" Mrs. Carter asked.

"Some kind of animal nailed to a joist."

"Nailed? Who would do such a thing?"

"I wonder."

$\mathcal{S}$asha called this morning. She had seen Julia, who sent her love. Cordelia hadn't seen Julia in years, not since she decided Cordelia would never marry any of the men she set her up with. Their lives had grown apart. Sometimes that happens.

Sasha told Cordy she just wanted to call to check and see if she was still alive. It made her smile. Few things make Cordelia smile anymore. Sometimes even the tiny gesture of changing a facial expression is just too much effort. The radio receiver has a remote control so she can change channels. One finger is all you need to find a new song. She surfs the frequencies to find a comforting sound, a song to remind her of the past, or maybe the voice of God. A singer interested in the dying. Gabrielle has to turn down the volume because Cordy can reach the up volume button but can rarely find the down. Twenty-one stations are programmed into the receiver. Cordy handles the remote as if she is a contestant on "Name That Tune"—no station ever stays on for more than seven notes. Marconi plays the mamba . . .

$\mathcal{I}$ miss classical radio. There is no classical station on my receiver, only oldies stations. It is hard to imagine that there are that many oldies out there. I have no objection to hearing music from the fifties and sixties, but I would like to hear some music from now. I have a station that specializes in music of the fifties and sixties, one that plays your favorite hits from the sixties, music from the sixties and seventies, I am lost in the land of the oldies. There are just so many times one can hear "96 Tears." Soon there will be stations that play only covers of original hits. There will be the all-Elvis station and the all-Elvis cover station and the all-tribute station. I miss Liz Phair and Counting Crows.

*A*ll the oldies make Cordelia depressed. When she is depressed she thinks of Julia. When she thinks of Julia, she thinks of Miles Evans III. Miles Evans III walks. He walks everywhere. There isn't a road between Equality and Sylacauga that he hasn't walked. Miles started walking when he was twelve. His family didn't let him out of the house much. Then one day, he stepped off the porch and started walking around town. I guess he wanted to see what he hadn't seen all those years inside. When he took to the roads, nobody was surprised, because everyone knew he was a little off. Cordelia never heard him talk, though there was no reason that he couldn't. Maybe he was like the chimps. Maybe he didn't have anything to say, but he did walk.

Often people gave him rides. The fifth Cordelia gave him rides, and Cordelia's mother gave him rides from the time Cordelia was a child. The short rides were welcomed, though they never got him to his destination, since that place was locked somewhere inside of him.

When Cordelia went away to school, she ended up with Julia as a roommate. Julia grew up believing that the center of the universe was located in New York City in an area that was bordered by Fifth and Park Avenues between Seventy-seventh and Eighty-seventh. As Cordelia told stories of Alabama, Julia grew more amazed at this strange place. Julia had traveled to Europe and Africa, but in all her travels, she had never heard of a more exotic band of people, and her insatiable appetite for stories caused Cordelia to stretch the truth and eventually wander into fantasy. After graduation, Julia looked for an apartment in New York while Cordelia came home to visit. In a few days, she called to say she had found an apartment on the corner of Columbus Avenue and Seventy-eighth Street. Cordelia realized the apartment was directly across Central Park from where she had grown up, a dramatic step toward independence. She also informed Cordelia that she was bored and she was coming to visit.

"It's time I saw Alabama. Shall I fly into Birmingham or Montgomery?"

Cordelia picked her up in Birmingham, and for a week they traveled country roads in search of adventure. The fifth Cordelia cooked grits and cornbread and once she cooked squirrel.

"It reminds me of rabbit I ate in the South of France."

Cordelia told her interesting facts. Sylacauga is Indian for buzzard's roost. The quarry is the largest open-pit marble quarry in the world. She showed her Willy-Nilly, the two-headed snake that had met his maker years before, though he's still attracting crowds at the Goodwater Barbershop. Cordelia took her to her father's grave in the new cemetery, her grandfather's grave in the old cemetery, and her great-grandparents' grave in Clay County.

"My grandparents are scattered somewhere off the Cape."

Their last stop was the house where her mother was born. It was occupied by an elderly black couple, Mattie and Samuel, who once worked for the fifth Cordelia. Samuel showed Julia his prized possession, Omar, a twenty-seven-pound possum. Cordelia told her the opossum is North America's only native marsupial.

"Can they be housebroken?"

They stopped in Equality to get Julia's luggage and to say good-bye. Driving back toward the Birmingham airport, they saw Miles Evans III walking toward Sylacauga. He wore his usual uniform of dark pants, white shirt, skinny tie, and glasses. Cordelia pulled the car over.

"What are you doing?"

Cordelia told her she was picking up Miles, explaining that he was a fixture in the community and assuring her that they would be all right.

"I wouldn't pick up a nun. Besides, he looks like Anthony Perkins."

Miles walked to the car, never changing his steady gait, and got in the back. Cordelia carried on the conversation for all three of them, telling Miles he looked like Anthony Perkins and telling Miles about Julia's travels in Europe. They didn't take the four-lane, but drove the back road across Hatchet Creek and past Parkdale. Julia sat erect, her hands folded in her lap, with her eyes often glancing toward the passenger in the backseat. Miles sat erect, looking out the window at the foliage whipping by. When they reached Sylacauga, Cordelia let Miles out of the car by the service station. He nodded thanks and walked off toward down-town.

At the airport, the attendant announced they were ready to board. As Julia disappeared through the gate she was still talking.

"Coliseums and ruins don't seem like much once you've seen a twenty-seven-pound opossum."

Cordelia shared the apartment with Julia until Julia decided to get married. She chose an attractive, slightly older, extremely boring investment banker and they moved to the Upper East Side. For several years, twice a year, Cordelia went to their apartment for dinner. At each dinner Cordelia was seated across the table from an attractive, boring investment banker. After dinner, standing on the balcony, Julia would ask what she thought of him, how she liked him, and Cordelia would always say the same thing—he's an investment banker.

"What's it going to take to get you to marry one?"

Cordelia told her perhaps she would marry an investment banker if Julia would find one who owned a twenty-seven-pound opossum.

When I am depressed I think of Julia on the Upper East Side and of Miles Evans III walking the roads of Alabama. They are both doing what they do best. That is all you can ask.

Chalcedony grows after the sun has set and the air is still a lit-tle warm. It gets its warmth more from the air than from the sun. Whoever wishes to possess eloquence and art, to choose the right word while speaking, take the chalcedony in your hand and breathe on it so that it becomes covered with moisture. Then lick this moisture with your tongue and you will be eloquent.

*W*hen she was forty-two years old, almost forty-three, Hildegard von Bingen was consumed with a life-threatening disease. She saw a burning light of tremendous brightness coming from heaven, and the light poured into her entire mind, like a flame that didn't burn but enkindled. She said of the light that it inflamed her entire heart and breast, like the sun that warms an object with its rays. All at once she was able to taste of the understanding of books. The burning light redeemed Hildegard, who would live to be eighty-one. In her second life, she would compose seventy-seven liturgical songs. Today the songs have been transposed and arranged, accompanied by musicians and singers, digitized and pressed on compact disks.

If you hold it just right, the tiny silver disk will catch the light and reflect it like a flame. Songs and flames on one tiny disk. What would Hildegard think of such a thing. Digitized music. Does it sound different on a disk? Does it look different? Are there CDs in heaven? Maybe I will ask her after I talk to Janis. Hildegard wrote several volumes of visions and prophecies, studies on nature and medicine, and would lose the sacraments of the Church for refusing to exhume the corpse of a man whom she buried on hallowed ground. The Church wanted the infidel moved, but Hildegard refused, saying he had confessed to her and therefore died with grace. Hildegard won the battle, and by the year's end she was buried in that same cemetery.

Lick the moisture with your tongue and you will be eloquent.

I am waiting for the burning light.

ook, Cordelia, we had snow."

"It doesn't look like snow."

"Feel how cold it is. Feel my hands. It's snow. Maybe not like that New York snow you're used to, but it's snow. Hell, another six or eight days like this and we could make a snowman."

"We don't have that long."

"Don't be a quitter, Cordelia."

"Can you see her?"

"Who?"

"It's me—floating."

"Floating?"

"I can touch the ceiling. Jeanette Winterson said art celebrates ceilings and denies floors. If she's right, then perhaps death is the last great art form. From here I can see everything. What's the capital of Gambia?"

"Why?"

"You'll need to know."

"Why?"

"You're dying."

"I thought all I needed was Last Rites."

"Only if you're Catholic. You're not, are you?"

"I'm not religious."

"It's not religious, it's geographic. At the end they ask you capitals. You'll need to know."

asha believed her when she told her about the cancer.

Sasha believed the New York doctor when he said it would be no longer than three months.

Sasha ordered the packers for the books that went to Matthew.

Sasha closed up the apartment in the Village.

Sasha took her clothes to the Goodwill.

Sasha helped pick out the black wool suit with the pleated pants.

Sasha drove her to Equality.

Sasha went with her to the lawyer and watched her sign a living will.

Sasha watched her sign a Do Not Resuscitate form.

Sasha sat beside her at the funeral home.

Sasha kissed her good-bye as though she would see her again.

Sasha walked out the door and failed to heed the warning given to Lot's wife.

Sasha looked back.

*I*s it a boy or a girl?"

"I don't know."

"Didn't you have the test?"

"I had amniocentesis, but I didn't want to know, but I'll know soon."

"What do you want?"

"A healthy baby. I don't care. My husband wants a boy."

"Men are like that. Would you want to know when you're going to die?"

"Nope."

"I went to a psychic."

"What did she tell you?"

"I was in for major changes after I turned thirty. I guess I got my money's worth. Remember the story about Augusta?"

"No."

"I told you about her going to prison. She went to sing and they kept her, remember?"

"No. It must have been Dr. Campbell. But tell me anyway."

"Augusta went to a psychic. Madame Duvalier. Madame Duvalier knows all."

*T*he wooden sign with the flaking paint became visible in the distance. It bore a single word: READER. Mary Elizabeth, her sister Rachael, and their cousin, Augusta, had arrived at Madame Duvalier's.

They had gone to Madame Duvalier's because Mary Elizabeth was bored with her life. She had watched most of the young men she knew join the army to fight in Europe. Those who had stayed behind, cowards like Dickie Reed and Calvin Jakes, were not worth wasting her time. She had longed to be in the thick of the war effort at exotic places comforting wounded heroes, but the best she could do was to work in the powder plant and dream that a young soldier would save his platoon with ammunition that she had made. Desperate for excitement, Mary Elizabeth had planned the adventure.

"We're going on an adventure," Mary Elizabeth said to Augusta and Rachael.

"What kind of an adventure?" asked Augusta.

"We're going to see the reader," Mary Elizabeth answered as she smiled a smile that always got someone into trouble. "Not afraid, are you?"

Augusta and Rachael shook their heads an unconvincing no, but Mary Elizabeth knew they had lied, and their apprehension delighted her.

Madame Duvalier was the local mystic. It was not known why she came to Equality from New Orleans, but she quickly became a local fixture. In her most famous case, she had led the police to the body of a child who had been missing for weeks by merely touching the boy's teddy bear. Many people had visited Madame Duvalier to hear their future, though few would admit to such dabbling into the occult.

Now, standing on the steps of the reader's house, Mary Elizabeth made a fist and knocked on the door with one sharp rap, causing the screen to vibrate in its frame and Augusta and Rachael to jump to a lower step.

"Come in," a voice filtered from another part of the house. "I be with you in a bit."

Mary Elizabeth opened the door slowly, accentuating a small squeak. Augusta entered first, and as Rachael crossed the threshold, her sister whispered, "Watch for bats."

The girls were disappointed with the decor of the living room. It was bright and airy. There were no skulls or cobwebs as they had expected. The only thing black was a pillow with NEW ORLEANS embroidered on it in red thread. There was an overstuffed couch and two chairs, a small table, several plants, and the brick-a-brac that one collects during a lifetime. The fireplace was closed and a large glass planter sat empty on the floor in front of it.

Mary Elizabeth walked to the mantle to look at a doll. It was a small whisk broom about six inches high. Its skirt was made of broom straw, the torso was round wood painted bright red with yellow buttons and a crisp yellow collar; it had no arms. Sitting on top of the torso was a round wooden head, half red for the cap, half black for the face. The face bore a red mouth, a white nose, and the whites of two eyes, and carried the forlorn look of someone deformed and doomed to spend her life brushing lint.

Mary Elizabeth looked left and right, and as her companions watched, she unceremoniously spit into the planter, raised her hand, and touching her forehead in a gesture fit for Tallulah Bankhead, said, "Let's see if she knows."

Within seconds the curtains parted at the end of the living room. It was Madame Duvalier in the flesh. She, too, was somewhat of a disappointment to the girls. As with the decor of the living room, they had expected something wild and exotic. They had visions of a woman in prints and hundreds of gold bangles. Instead, the woman wore a simple black dress, and the only thing remotely mysterious was a print scarf that wrapped her head. She moved toward the fireplace and stood facing Mary Elizabeth, never taking her eyes from her.

"I be Madame Duvalier," she said, and pointing her toe she slid the glass planter an inch. "Oughta plant me something in this planter, don't you think?" Her eyes were still fixed on Mary Elizabeth's eyes.

The reader turned her attention to Augusta and Rachael as they stood transfixed. Her manner became more outgoing as she took Augusta's hand.

"You be Miss Augusta."

Then she turned her attention to Rachael, whose eyes must have widened as Madame Duvalier stepped closer and took her hand. The reader cocked her head back, laughed a deep laugh, and said, "You eyes pop! Like popcorn."

While Madame Duvalier held Rachael's hand, she kept her eyes on the girl's older sister. With a sudden jerk that mimicked Mary Elizabeth's movements at the planter, the reader raised her hand to her forehead and in a low staccato voice said, "You be Miss Rachael," and she laughed deeply as she turned to face Mary Elizabeth, who didn't miss a beat and said to the reader, "And I be Miss Mary Elizabeth." A second passed without a sound and then, simultaneously, they all began to laugh.

Madame Duvalier took Mary Elizabeth's hand and the smile momentarily left her face. She held the pale, delicate hand as though it were hot, as though she wanted to drop it. She held on. A different smile returned. Quickly turning, she said, "Time enough for two readings. You two." She looked at Augusta and Rachael. Augusta stepped forward and followed Madame Duvalier behind the curtains. Mary Elizabeth and Rachael waited for what seemed to them to be an hour, but was actually closer to five minutes. Augusta came back to the parlor and told Rachael it was now her turn.

Rachael entered the small room that had probably been a porch at one time. It was dark, though not dark enough to prevent her from seeing. A hutch stood against one wall. It was filled with cups and saucers of every description. A table stood in the center of the room with a starched linen tablecloth, and the air hung heavy with the aroma of spices.

"Pick you a cup," Madame Duvalier said.

She picked a delicate cup, white with a tiny yellow bird on it. The cup rattled against the saucer as she took it down from the hutch and she prayed that it would not break. It was made of a fine bone china, the kind that rings like a bell when tapped with your fingernail. Rachael set it on the table, and Madame Duvalier dropped in some tea leaves and covered them with steaming water. They talked for a while in much the same manner one would talk to a Sunday school teacher.

Rachael drank some of the tea and then Madame Duvalier poured off the remaining liquid and peered down into the cup at the leaves. She told her that she would do a lot of traveling and Rachael asked if perhaps Madame Duvalier had gotten Mary Elizabeth's tea leaves by mistake. After all, she had never traveled farther than the Florida panhandle in her life. The reader told her that she would marry someone from the West. The farthest west Rachael had ever gone was Birmingham, and she had met no likely candidates for marriage. Finally, she told her that she would have two children and one of them would be a girl. The reading was over. As Rachael started to leave, Madame Duvalier touched her shoulder and in a voice almost inaudible she whispered, "You be growing up real soon."

The return from Madame Duvalier's lacked the death march quality of the trip to her house. As they returned home, a red sky engulfed Equality. Stopping on the bridge overlooking the train tracks, they listened to the slow whistle of a distant train. As the whistle faded, the girls realized the day was gone. Mary Elizabeth and Rachael parted company with Augusta and went home. Rachael wanted to go to bed and sleep the night away, but she and her sister had to get ready for Sunday.

Rachael loved church, and thought about the ritual as she ironed the clothes for Sunday morning. She liked to dress up and to talk with friends. The sounds of the pipe organ and the flowers and the candles made her happy. Her religious fervor was disrupted by Mary Elizabeth.

"What is this?" she asked as she held up her blouse, warm from the iron.

"Your blouse," Rachael said. Mary Elizabeth laughed a disgusted laugh and took the iron from her younger sister's hand, pulling her away from the ironing board and shoving her toward the couch. Mary Elizabeth's voice rang out with its usual candor, "You can't do anything right."

Sitting on the couch, Rachael watched her sister. Next to church, she liked watching Mary Elizabeth most of all. There was a rhythm to Mary Elizabeth, a beauty in the most simple actions. Her hands were long and slender and they moved freely in the folds of the clothes she ironed. She knew where to fold the fabric and how to hold the iron to get to all the tiny creases. The buttons sat up off the material as she pressed around each pearl circle, and the lace around the collar seemed to dance. When she hung the blouse on the hanger, it appeared to hold the body of the wearer within it.

She continued to watch Mary Elizabeth iron. There was none of the familiar drudgery as she hung the newly pressed clothes about the room until she appeared to have an audience. The heat from the iron gave a gentle flush to Mary Elizabeth's cheeks, and her red hair cascaded in soft curls to frame her face. Rachael had never wished to be as beautiful as Mary Elizabeth nor as bright nor adventurous; her only wish was that one day she would be able to do the simple things with the poise and ease with which Mary Elizabeth did everything.

The house was bustling with Sunday-morning activity when Rachael awoke. As usual, Mary Elizabeth's bed was empty and neatly made. Only when she awoke in the night did she find Mary Elizabeth in the bed, for her sister was always the last one to go to bed and the first one to get up. Mary Elizabeth believed that sleep was a waste of time. Just once, Rachael had wished to wake up before her sister.

Rachael stumbled to the kitchen to help Mary Elizabeth with breakfast, their regular Sunday-morning chore. As Rachael stood in the door frame of the kitchen yawning, Mary Elizabeth did not speak, but merely imitated the yawn and smiled her mischievous smile. All the ingredients for breakfast lay neatly arranged on the counter. There was really no need for Rachael to be present since breakfast was in capable hands.

She watched Mary Elizabeth's hands lift the eggs and crack them into a china bowl, the delicate white hands gingerly cradling the eggs, the shell breaking against the white bowl rim, the egg sliding to the bottom and hitting with a soft ring. Mary Elizabeth, realizing that she had an audience, took the next egg with more force, and holding it in the palm of her left hand, she cracked it hard against the bowl and separated the shell in a single motion. Without missing a beat she curled her hand like a pitcher and tossed the shell to Rachael, who missed the shells. They landed on the floor at her feet.

Stooping to retrieve the shells, Rachael looked up and saw Mary Elizabeth lift a kitchen match from the box and hold it as though it were a conductor's baton. Her motion was fluid as she raked the match over the bricks by the window. The sound was familiar; rough scratching, quiet popping and a hiss, followed by the pungent smell of sulfur. Rachael returned to the shells, knowing the next sound would be the whoosh of the burner igniting.

There was no whoosh. Rachael heard an unfamiliar sound as though someone had filled a paper bag with air and popped it close to her ear. She looked at Mary Elizabeth. The smile remained on her face and Rachael was comforted by it, so comforted that the gravity of the situation did not sink in. Even as she watched the ball of fire climb the sleeve of her sister's robe, Rachael's only thought was how the flames matched the color of Mary Elizabeth's hair. And then the smile was gone.

Mary Elizabeth fled from the kitchen and burst into the yard. Rachael followed her because she had always followed Mary

Elizabeth. She stopped only momentarily to throw the eggshells into the trash basket. In the light of the morning, she could see Mary Elizabeth lying on the ground. Seeing the black contours of her body and the blackness of the ground around her, Rachael was sorry that she had not thought to bring this blanket for Mary Elizabeth, but she disliked the choice of a black blanket.

When she reached Mary Elizabeth, she tried to lift the blanket but it did not exist. She turned the body over to be comforted by her sister's smile, but there was no comfort. She screamed her name but there was no sound, only silence.

Augusta's face was the next thing that Rachael saw.

"You're at my house now." Augusta pulled her close, trying without success to comfort her. Rachael wouldn't go home, and in the two days that followed the fire, she could do nothing but blame herself for the accident. Replaying the events of the fire over a million times, she kept coming to the same conclusion. If she had been on fire and Mary Elizabeth had been picking up the shells, they would both be alive. Mary Elizabeth could have saved her, but Rachael couldn't save Mary Elizabeth. The more she thought about it, the more she pondered the notion that the trip to Madame Duvalier's had contributed to Mary Elizabeth's death. She couldn't sleep or eat.

After the funeral, Augusta drove Rachael home, choosing a circuitous route so that she would avoid seeing the charred yard. Stepping up onto the porch, Rachael froze. Suddenly the door came open and several of the ladies from the church whisked her into the house. As Augusta followed, all she could think of in the crowd of mourners was how amused Mary Elizabeth would have been by all of this and how wicked her comments would have been.

Rachael was being led too close to the kitchen and Augusta tried to rescue her. Before she could get to her, Rachael found herself standing alone before the dining room table, which was laden with food the Sunday school class had prepared for the mourners. The ladies began to pull dish towels off the food like magicians in a frenzy. There were cakes and pies, fruits and vegetables, and as the last cloth was lifted, it revealed a whole baked ham. As the steam rose from the meat, Rachael began to look faint. Augusta's quick reflexes saved her from falling to the floor.

Augusta rocked the porch swing, trying to comfort Rachael as she wept, but she could not be consoled. In her grief, she failed to notice the sound of footsteps coming up the stairs of the porch until the figure stood before her. When she looked up, she saw Madame Duvalier.

Madame Duvalier reached out to touch Rachael's head but the girl resisted, digging her heels into the porch floor and pushing the swing back as far as it would go. Madame Duvalier stepped back, nodded, and moved to the door. Letting go of the swing suddenly, Rachael let it jerk forward, startling Augusta. She raised her hand and in a strong voice called out to the reader, "Did you do it?"

The figure at the door slowly turned, extending her hands toward Rachael's hand, which was quickly pulled away. She laughed a quiet laugh, almost a sigh, and facing Rachael with arms outstretched, palms upward, the reader began to speak.

"I have a gift. I touch your clothes . . . I touch your toys . . . I feel you. I see faces and places and I know. Good and bad. I touch your hands . . . I see your past and your future." She knelt before Rachael. "I touch Mary Elizabeth's hands . . . they have no future."

Rachael took the reader's hands as she stood erect. "The power be bigger than me, bigger than you. No one be stopping it." She stroked the girl's cheek. The tone in her voice changed as she broke into a familiar smile. "You and Augusta . . . you got big futures."

Augusta stood to open the door for the reader. Madame Duvalier smiled at Augusta and winked at Rachael as she entered the house. Sitting back down in the swing, Augusta stroked Rachael's hair as it lay on her shoulder. Rachael was calm for the first time in days. The rusty chains of the porch swing squeaked in rhythm as they rocked, and the warm wind of the Alabama evening blew in quiet absolution.

$\mathcal{B}$anjul."

"Bonjour to you, Doctor."

"No Banjul. The capital of Gambia."

"Do you see her now?"

"Yes, I do, and she bears a most striking resemblance to you. You could be twins, or one and the same."

"What are you doing up there, Dr. Campbell?"

"Denying the floor and celebrating the ceiling. Floating. Leaving. You won, Cordelia."

"I wasn't playing."

"And you still won. But I know all the capitals."

"Go in peace. The Lord is with you."

"And also with you."

DR. JAMES MCKINEY CAMPBELL

EQUALITY—Dr. James McKiney Campbell, 83, died of cancer at his home. He was a lifelong resident of Equality. Dr. Campbell was a graduate of the University of Alabama and Duke University Medical School. He practiced medicine for over 50 years until his retirement five years ago. His grandson, Byron McKiney Campbell, Jr., took over the practice.

In addition to the young Dr. Campbell, he is survived by a son, Dr. Byron McKiney Campbell, Sr., of Birmingham, a daughter, Mrs. Steven Arthur Pike of

Opelika, six grandchildren, and four great-grandchildren.

Reed / Thomas Funeral home will be handling the arrangements. The service will be held Sunday at 2:00 p.m. at the First Methodist Church. In lieu of flowers, the family has requested that donations be made to the American Cancer Society.

$\mathcal{D}$o you always leave the door open like that? Some psycho could come in and kill you."

"I was hoping. What are you doing here, Matthew? I told you not to come."

"I was just in the neighborhood and thought . . ."

"What a lame answer."

"I just had to see you one . . . again."

"Go ahead and say it, babe. One last time. Besides, we already had one last time. I took you to 21. That was supposed to be that."

"You're as hard as Sasha."

"We're both pragmatists. How are the books?"

"God, my apartment looks like Barnes and Noble. But I wish you hadn't."

"They're like my children. I wasn't sending them to foster care. I knew you'd look after them and love them. Like I did."

"God, it is like children."

$\mathcal{P}$oor Matthew doesn't know what to do. He sits by the bed looking distraught. This is exactly what Cordelia did not want. She tried so hard to clean up all the loose ends. She had buried both of her parents, her grandparents, two friends from AIDS. The hardest part was after. After the death and the funeral, after the wake and the interment, after all the people were gone and it was just you standing in a house or apartment filled with all the accumulations of a lifetime.

The funeral was the easy part.

The furniture was easy.

The clothes were easy.

The dishes and glasses were easy.

The car was easy.

What wasn't easy was all the little stuff that ended up in a pile in one last room. The odds and ends that were too good to throw away, but had no place in anyone's life anymore. There was always a pile of change, quarters, nickels, pennies. There was always a shiny tin that had once held cookies or fruitcake, or brownies. The embossed lid fit tightly on the can and when it came off, after a broken fingernail, the inside smelled as though it were still filled. There were always pictures with no notes written on the back, so you spent an hour guessing who was in them.

Who is this person?

What beach is this?

What party is this?

Whose baby is this?

And there is never anyone to answer the questions. Why did someone I loved hold on to these snapshots? One of the pictures always catches your eye. You think about it for years afterward. You can't quit asking.

When her grandfather died, Cordelia found a pocketknife. One of the blades was broken. Cordelia wanted to know why it was broken. How did it happen? What was he doing when he broke it? She held it in her hand and she could feel his hand on the knife. After years and years of holding it, peeling apples, whittling sticks, a part of him must still be there—some slight traces of DNA clinging to the knife as she held it in her hand. She could feel his heart beating.

Her grandmother had a necklace sent to her from a missionary in South Korea. All the years Lillian Wilson had taught school at the Methodist mission in Korea, the fifth Cordelia sent her money and prayed for her safety. Every night she prayed, even after the faithful had given up hope. Miss Wilson was captured by the North Koreans during the war and sent on a forced march that killed many of the captives. The church was convinced she was dead, but Cordelia's grandmother never stopped praying for her return. After the war, Miss Wilson was found, but she never talked about what happened to her, though the stories of the torture and abuse of prisoners were well documented. Her health was shattered, but her spirit was never daunted, and she never forgot that one person remained steadfast in the face of doubt. When she died, her niece sent a necklace of carved ivory to Cordelia's grandmother—a remembrance for never giving up hope. Only Cordelia knew the story, and now it will die with her.

Every room left behind is filled with profoundly important objects but the finder doesn't know why. When Brian died of AIDS, Cordelia made all the arrangements. She knew his body would cremate and the feather boa would cremate, but no one knew if his favorite Dior earrings would cremate. When she went to gather the ashes, the funeral director told Cordelia he was afraid to cremate the earrings. "I put them in a small velvet bag with his rosary. I'm afraid he rattles a little bit." Cordelia held the urn, and as she walked, she could hear the faint rattle of the rosary hitting the earrings as if he were whispering to her.

She set the urn on the floor of his apartment and gathered the remnants of a life. She found:

A strip of pictures from a photo booth with an unknown friend.

Three dollars and seventy-two cents in change.

A kazoo.

A baby picture in a small plastic frame.

Seven pens and four pencils.

A postcard of the *Isenheim Altarpiece*.

A pair of dice.

Three joints and a hemostat.

A lighter with a picture of Elvis.

Mardi Gras beads.

An empty tin that, judging from the smell, held chocolate chip cookies.

A roll of film waiting to be taken.

She arranged and rearranged the articles on the floor, putting them in a trash bag, then removing them.

She threw away the pencils, but she noticed they had teeth prints. Brian's teeth prints.

She held the postcard from the *Isenheim Altarpiece*. Brian sent her a card just like it. He referred to the image of Jesus as the Christ of Kaposi's Sarcoma.

She couldn't throw away Elvis.

She was afraid to throw away the joints and decided to flush them down the toilet, but instead she grabbed Elvis and lit up.

She rolled the dice and put on the beads.

She wished Brian had left just one cookie in the tin.

She held Brian in her lap and listened to him rattle.

Cordelia decided that what people needed was to hear the rattle. The government wasn't serious about AIDS, complaining that they didn't have enough money for research. She packed all of Brian's possessions into the cookie tin—his picture as a child and the ones from the photo booth, Elvis, the dice, the Christ of Kaposi's Sarcoma, the kazoo, $3.72, and she wrote a note in bold block letters:

TO WHOM IT MAY CONCERN:

THIS IS WHAT'S LEFT OF MY DEAR FRIEND BRIAN. ME-
MENTOS FROM HIS LIFE, A PICTURE OF HIM AS A CHILD
AND HIS LAST DIME. PLEASE ACCEPT THIS $3.72 AND USE
IT TO HELP FIND A CURE FOR AIDS.

Cordelia taped up the tin, which made an awful racket, Brian's rage against the dying of the light. Affixing a mailing label addressed to the National Institutes of Health, she gave Brian a last say; he would not suffer the silence of the grave, but become a raucous and noisy ghost, rattling through the post office and down the halls of the NIH. They, whoever "they" might be, would hear him coming and sit up and take notice.

What would happen, she wondered, if this became the norm for the disposal of possessions. A manual could be devised and distributed to funeral homes everywhere with preprinted address labels for charities and research organizations. It would be an alternative for everyone who had ever had to clean up an apartment, anyone who had ever had to throw away the last possessions of a loved one, anyone who felt helpless in the face of death, to give that person one last chance to make a stand. Thousands of men, women, and children dying, each with a name, a picture, a tin filled with change, all screaming in unison as the postal trucks dropped off the mementos and the money.

When Cordelia dies, they will find an envelope filled with pictures of Lee Radziwill. They will flip through the old magazine clippings and wonder why she kept them all these years. Then they will throw them in the fire as the flames curl the edges and Lee Radziwill and Rudolph Nureyev share one last kiss.

*Y*ou were asleep."
"I find it harder and harder to stay awake."
"I don't know what to say, Cordy."
"Don't say anything, just read to me."

> *I celebrate myself, and sing myself,*
> *And what I assume, you shall assume,*
> *For every atom belonging to me as good belongs to you. . . .*

"Are you glad I came?"
"Yes, I am."
"Do you want me to stay?"

"No. I want you to go home."

"I could read some more poetry."

"Go home, Matthew."

"What, my visit wasn't exciting enough?"

"Are you kidding? I haven't been this excited since the carnival came to town."

$\mathcal{T}$he multicolored Ferris wheel decorated a bright and glossy poster in the window of Carter's Hardware. It heralded the exciting news that the carnival was coming to Equality. It would be the biggest event in the town since the chicken truck ran the stoplight and turned over in front of the Shiloh Baptist Church. Buddy ran home to tell his mother. He found her sitting at the kitchen table watching Pearl cook. As long as Buddy could remember, his mother had been sickly, always looking pale and weak.

"The carnival's coming," Buddy yelled.

"Waste of good money," huffed Pearl, who had grown up with Buddy's grandmother, raised his mother, raised Buddy, and if Buddy had children she would probably raise them. They had always been together, and they always would be.

When Buddy was ready for bed, he lay quietly waiting for his mother to come and tuck him in. It was the same thing each night since his fifth birthday. He would lie flat on his back, the cover pulled over his head, toes pointed toward the closet. His heart would pound, and he would listen for her footsteps coming lightly up the stairs. She would enter the room and move toward the closet doors. His heart would pound harder. She tried to open them quietly, but they always made a low, scraping sound, then slid shut, he thought, like a coffin closing. Her presence would move to the side of the bed and the crisp white sheet would be folded away from his face. Each would smile and wink, and she would lay Emmylou beside him.

"Don't tell," she would whisper as she touched her lips to his cheek and disappeared down the hall. When he had turned five his father had said that boys did not play with dolls. He took Emmylou away, but each night since then his mother would slip the doll to him. Each morning she would hide it in the closet. It was their deepest secret. Only once had the ritual been broken.

He had gone to bed as usual. He waited, his toes pointed until his arches ached and cramped. He peered out from under the covers, but his mother never came. There were no stars in the sky, only darkness. He rolled to his side, tucking his knees to his chest, pulling his pillow close, though it was little consolation for Emmylou.

He tossed and turned, then awoke. It was not morning. The sky was still black, but the rest of the house seemed unusually bright. Buddy climbed out of bed and tiptoed down the red-carpeted stairs, down the back hall, and into the well-lit kitchen. He was startled. He saw Pearl, but he had never seen her without a rag tied around her head. Her cornrows were tightly woven, held by the red elastic that circled the morning papers. As he inched forward he saw the stove open, and Pearl was tending a box sitting on the oven rack. It was the white Sam Crew shoe box that his father's black loafers had come in. Buddy was mad that there had never been an extra shoe box when he wanted it, but Pearl had gotten one. As he inched closer, his eyes became fixed upon the contents of the box.

The baby lay swaddled in the box. She was tiny, no bigger than his father's hand. His mother had told him the baby would come between Thanksgiving and Christmas, and it wasn't even Halloween. She told Buddy he could name the baby. He knew it would be a girl, and he wanted to name her after his doll, Emmylou. His mother suggested "Emma," and after gentle persuasion, he agreed. Buddy rubbed his eyes, then moved closer for a better view. The tiny head was turned in his direction. She was small, but her eyes were big. She had their mother's gentle gray eyes, and though he had not meant to say anything, the words just slipped out.

"Emma," he whispered in a voice he thought was inaudible but which Pearl heard.

"Why is Emma in the oven?" he questioned.

Pearl had spent the last few hours assisting with the birth. Now she was trying to preserve the tiny life in the shoe box. She had puffed air into the undeveloped lungs and softly rubbed the skin to keep the blood flowing. The oven was the only constant source of heat in the house and Pearl now used it as an incubator. All these facts buzzed in her head, but none of them would answer a child. Nothing she might say could explain what was happening. She finally spoke to Buddy.

"Keeping it warm."

"Her, not it. Her!" he yelled.

"Get upstairs, boy," Pearl said in a voice that he had never heard. Something was wrong, and he climbed the stairs like a scolded pup, head down, tail between his legs.

As he topped the stairs, he looked toward his mother's room. A soft light fell on the worn carpet and he tiptoed toward it. She was in bed, asleep, he thought, as he moved toward her. She turned, and he saw her face which was sad and tearful.

"I saw Emma," he whispered. Her face was pale as he spoke to her. "Emma's beautiful."

"They won't let me see her." His mother's voice was weak. "Tell me, Buddy, is she all right? Does she have . . . Is she . . ."

Buddy began to tell her everything, trying hard to recall every detail of the baby in the box.

As morning burst through the windows, Buddy ran down the stairs. He looked all around the kitchen, and when Pearl found him he was looking in the oven.

"What are you doing?" Pearl called out, and he jumped like he had been shot, and if his head had been farther in the oven he would have surely cracked his skull.

"Looking for Emma," he said.

"God, child, you don't put babies in the oven."

"You did last night!"

"I was trying to keep it warm. . . ."

"Her!" he insisted, and Pearl saw that she was only upsetting the boy. She laid her strong hand on his blond head and guided him to the kitchen table.

"The baby's gone to be with Jesus." She began searching for words to explain death.

"She just couldn't breathe, and Jesus took her to be with him. Your father took her to the cemetery for a proper burial. . . ."

"In the Sam Crew box?"

"You don't bury babies in a shoe box. . . ."

"We buried Rusty in a shoe box," he insisted.

"Rusty was a kitten." Her voice rose, but she fought to calm it. "They gave her a proper burial. All God's children deserve a proper burial. Deep in the ground, so they can be with God."

He had more questions, but he did not ask them.

"Did you let my mother see Emma?" he asked softly, walking out of the kitchen.

"Don't you mention that again, boy!" Pearl's voice rose, and he never did.

The morning of the carnival Buddy could hardly sit still. After breakfast his mother laid out ten shiny dimes. He could spend them at the carnival, but when they were gone he would have to come home.

"Waste of good money," Pearl said. "He'll eat food I wouldn't feed an animal, spin round and round and get sick, and I'll be the one to look after him. I hear tell that one of them spinning things broke down in Mobile an' a bunch of——"

"Pearl!" his mother said in a sharp tone, and Pearl returned to her baking in the kitchen.

Equality was a small Alabama town where the kids walked to the carnival in the daytime, and the nights were reserved for the teenagers to court and the men to watch girlie dancers. "The biggest thing since the chicken truck," people said. True to Pearl's prediction, Buddy ate junk, rode on spinning things, and felt a bit sick. It was the last dime that changed things, the small piece of silver that altered the course of events that August day.

Buddy had won a genuine, made-in-Japan, plastic bear for his mother. He was so proud of the bear. He held it tightly and thought about his mother placing it on the Chippendale table next to the small blue vase with the tiny flowers painted on its side. Clutching the bear in one hand and the dime in the other, he thought about how he should spend his final coin. He came upon a huckster who sounded like the auctioneer he had heard at his grandfather's farm when they sold the soybeans.

Casting his eyes on the poster outside the tent, he saw the crude likeness of a boy about his own age. The figure of the boy was larger than life. The paint on the poster had faded in the sun. The boy wore short pants and saddle shoes and a strange shirt that allowed each of his three arms to be displayed. Buddy was filled with curiosity, the same kind he had felt when the neighbor's puppy was run over by the car. He gave the man his dime.

Entering the canvas tent, he could not see the boy. The air was heavy and dank, and he moved toward a table in the center of the tent. As he moved closer a sudden odor filled the air. It was unfamiliar to him, and the closest comparison he knew was in the fall when Pearl made dill pickles. His jaws ached, and his eyes and nose began to water as he moved closer.

A small card table stood in the center of the tent. On the table were old newspaper clippings, yellowed and tattered. One faded picture showed the three-armed boy playing baseball, while others displayed children with various physical malformations. On the corner of the table was a large jar. Buddy peered into it. He was not quite sure what he saw. He continued looking in the jar; the fluid, almost to the top, magnified the image within.

The sudden realization of what he was seeing filled him with an emotion that he could not define. The water continued to play tricks, and he thought the tiny head turned toward him. He was sure it looked at him, even though the eyes were closed. He felt like the pressure cooker whose valve had been put on incorrectly, the steam building until it exploded. Buddy exploded. He ran until he could no longer breathe. His mind flashed back to his mother's Emma. He remembered all the events of that night as though it were yesterday. He had always wanted to do something for Emma. Now, he had his chance.

Hurrying home from the carnival, he presented the bear to his mother. He talked of the carnival but quickly left the house to play. In the garage, he oiled the wheels of his old red wagon and loaded it with tools. He pulled it through the yard and far out back he began to dig. As supper time drew near, Pearl called out. "Come in here, Buddy. What are you doing out there?"

"Building a . . . dam," he responded.

"Looks like a hole to me," Pearl said. His mother smiled as he went upstairs to get ready for supper. "Children have such vivid imaginations, don't they, Pearl?"

That night was totally dark, and he fought his body which craved sleep. Finally it was time, he thought. He rose and dressed, and with Emmylou under his arm, he crept out of the house. He pulled the wagon into the street. For Emma, he thought. As the silent wheels turned, the clouds parted and the moon glowed brightly, lighting their path. Buddy knew in his heart that Emma had asked Jesus to part those clouds, and he grew more determined as he headed down the road to the carnival.

In the back of the green canvas tent his heart beat so loudly that he thought someone was walking behind him. He lay down and slid under the tent and felt his way to the flap he had seen earlier that day. It flipped open and the moon beamed right into the tent as if God were controlling a spotlight. Emma, he thought as he pulled the wagon into the tent.

Standing by the jar he found a new set of problems. He hadn't thought how heavy the jar would be or about getting caught or what would happen if he dropped the jar. Horror filled his body, and his teeth chattered as if he were stuck in a snowdrift, even though it must have been ninety degrees in the tent. His hands shook, and he started to leave. He gazed at the moon. "For Emma," he said aloud as he turned and loaded the jar onto the wagon.

The cortege moved down the back street with Emmylou, the rag-stuffed mourner, riding with the body. Soon they arrived at Buddy's yard. He gingerly lowered the jar into the hole. He worried that it was not deep enough because Pearl said that was important, but it was too late now. The dirt made a soft thud as it hit the jar. He worried that the child would be alone. Not knowing what made him do it, he lifted Emmylou from his wagon and laid her down beside the jar.

"You need her more than I do. You're scared, I bet." It seemed like the right thing to do. He filled the hole, packed the dirt, and parked the wagon on top. As he slipped into the house, the clouds filled the sky and darkness came again. He climbed into his bed to sleep.

The next morning, Buddy jumped from his bed and ran down the stairs, anxious to see his mother. Rounding the corner at top speed, he hit the Chippendale table, knocking over the Dresden vase. While his mother poured him a glass of orange juice, Pearl grabbed a dishrag and moved to clean up the boy's mess. Standing before the mirror that hung above the table she had waxed several days earlier, she set the vase upright, next to the bear. The sun hit the mirror and bounced around the room. The water that had fallen onto Pearl's wax was beading into drops, clear and round like the faces of children as she wiped them away.

dancing child with his Chinese suit. . . .

$\mathcal{T}$here is a certain eroticism in pain. I have always been fond of the simple, exquisite pain of the juice of a fresh lemon on a torn cuticle, fond of hot, salty popcorn on a chapped cut lip, fond of running my tongue over a canker sore close to the gum, fond of picking at scabs to reopen a wound. After the cancer, my body became a pariah. No one touched it but the cancer who took control like a dominating lover. The pain kissed my body and held it in endless fascination and turmoil.

What I miss the most is not the sex but the intimacy. The touch of a human hand. Matthew always greeted me with a hug and kiss, but the moment he heard about the cancer, he stopped touching me, waved hello and saluted good-bye. His arms which were often around my shoulder or waist hung foolishly at his sides. I suppose that I could have sympathized with his fears of touching my body, but I could never get used to his censorship of his language. Before we ever shared our bodies, we shared a love of the language. The formation of words, the syntax, the alliteration, the classic word or phrase that we read and reread to each other.

The day I told him of the cancer, it was as if the specter of the Hayes Code had risen from the grave. He never spoke of my body, never mentioned breasts or thighs, PMS or migraines, love or death or sex in the afternoon. He thought about every word before he said it. Never spoke with extemporaneous passion but always with a calculated cadence for fear he might go to jail if he misspoke.

In the *Isenheim Altarpiece*, Jesus is not really the Christ of Kaposi's sarcoma, he is the Christ of Ergotism, of Saint Anthony's Fire, of choreomania. Tainted rye. Bread from flour scraped from the bottom of the barrel. Moldy rye. The joints swell like arthritis. Sores cover the body. Vivid, wild hallucinations and finally death. Joan of Arc broke the bread. She saw the vivid image of Michael the Archangel. Michael of Ergotism. Joan burning before the dance.

There is but one way to ease the pain of Saint Anthony's Fire— to dance. The constant movement of the joints makes the pain bearable. I want constant movement. Once when she was aged, trapped in a body burning with arthritis, Martha Graham sat gingerly, explaining a movement to one of her dancers. Unable to find the words, she was helped to the stage, old and crippled. On the stage, in the glare of the spotlights, framed by the proscenium arch, nostrils filled with smell of the sweating dancers, ears filled with the faint strains of the musical score, Martha Graham danced. For one brief moment, the body was released and Martha Graham danced.

I want to dance.

I want any movement at all.

I want to drown my pain in dance.

I want to be Isadora on speed. Ecstatic dancing to drown the pain.

Drowning in the dance.

I would have been a brilliant Spanish dancer. But my body doesn't move.

Gabrielle is the only person who touches my body. I look forward to her visits and to the shots she brings, though I would never let her know. At first, I played games with the injections. I would count the shots with precision, hoping that my calculations might lead to a formula that would save me. Long before the capitals of the world, I was finding games for the shots. I would think of word puzzles to keep the clumps of shots together.

Two Gentlemen of Verona

Three Brontë Sisters.

Four horsemen of the Apocalypse.

Five great lakes, Huron, Ontario, Michigan, Erie, and

Superior, easy to remember because of the acronym
HOMES
Six Moral Tales of Eric Rohmer. Six mortal tales
Seven wonders of the world, both ancient and modern
Ten little Indians
Twelve days of Christmas
Twenty-two
Thirty-six
Forty-three

The numbers grew too big for any game or calculation. I was no engineer, no Einstein, no martyr to the cause, I would never be able to solve this problem in the time I have left.

The pain has become a kind of sex for me. The pain takes over my body like sex had always taken it over, but the pain is constant. My body stays hot and consumed, the cancer keeps me awake, it never sleeps like an oversexed lover, it won't leave my body alone, won't let me sleep, keeps me hot and bothered. Only the injections stop the constant foreplay of the illness. The injections like liquid fire, burning my veins and drowning the pain. Injections instead of the dance.

Gabrielle takes over from the tired lover. Her banter is the final act of foreplay before the injection. I play the game with all the foolishness of a young girl after a suitor. A woman with no self-worth, I will say anything to prolong the excitement, say anything to make Gabrielle stay, manipulate my language to say what she wanted to hear. I appear not to be as smart as I am. I don't want her to stop asking me the capitals. I tell her the shots hurt, knowing she will spend more time and care with the injection. I don't want this moment to end.

Gabrielle holds my hand, stroking my arm as she looks for a vein. Tying my arm just above the elbow with a thick elastic band, she tries to force the blood in my arm. She rolls the vein and flicks her index finger on my bare skin forcing the vein to the surface. Fluid bubbles out of the needle, and when she is sure the liquid is flowing, Gabrielle places the tip of the needle above the vein and pierces the skin, forcing the needle deep into my vein. Drowning me with fire.

I close my eyes and think of Saint Sebastion. There is only one Saint Sebastion for my taste in martyrdom. I only see Mangtena's *Saint Sebastion*. On my list of regrets I have added the failure to see the painting in the flesh, but I see the reproductions vividly. Sebastion's body is strong and muscular, the way my body once felt. Though he is bound to a column and has suffered the slings and arrows, he is remarkably calm, as though resigned to the injections of the arrows. The viewer is convinced that Sebastion will die from his injuries, but Sebastion is coy and reserved. He will not allow the viewer's pity to interfere with his pleasure.

Andrea Mantegna was born in 1431. Born in Isola di Cartura. I can feel the hard steel inside the vein, warmed and swollen from the friction of the needle. When the hot fluid mingles with the blood, the pain is calmed and I am frozen in time, drowned in the fire, suspended in never-never land. When I finally wake up, Gabrielle is gone.

Rome is the capital of Italy.

Cordelia, it's Gabrielle. I've brought someone to meet you. This is Anthony. He's going to be your nurse when I'm on maternity leave."

"Anthony."

"Nice to meet you, Cordelia."

"You were right, Cordelia, not all nurses are women. She accused me of being 'gender specific' when I referred to the new nurse as 'she.' "

"I'm a 'he,' and a dark one at that. Some of the patients are not too happy about that."

"Let them die."

"Oh, honey, you're a tough act to follow. Let's see if I can find a vein as quick as Gabby can."

"We play a game when I give her the shot. I ask her capitals and she answers. Like the capital of Turkey."

"Constantinople."

"Wrong. Besides, it's Istanbul now."

"Istanbul is the capital of Turkey."

"No. Constantinople is now Istanbul, but neither one is the capital of Turkey. It's Ankara."

"Anthony, did you study geography at nursing school?"

"No, honey, Constantinople was close enough for me."

*T*here was a time in America when the blood supply was segregated—black and white, Hebrew and Gentile. There is a story that President Eisenhower issued an Executive Order to integrate the blood supply. He was told that the South would never agree to the use of integrated blood. Eisenhower was said to have remarked, "If the South doesn't want integrated blood, then we won't send them any." Dr. Campbell remembered when it was like that.

There is a story that Dr. Charles Drew, the African-American doctor who invented the blood transfusion, was hurt in a car accident. He needed a blood transfusion and was taken to a hospital that would not admit Negroes. Charles Drew died for lack of a transfusion. His daughter says the story is a myth. Cordelia remembered when the fountain at the bus station said "Whites Only." Some patients don't want Anthony to be their nurse. There was a time when neither Dr. Drew nor Anthony could have been treated at the hospital in Equality. It was like the old fountain, "Whites Only."

*E*stes Jakes was a smart-ass. Being a smart-ass ran in the Jakes family like their black hair, which began to turn gray at the onset of puberty. Estes's best friend since grade school was Bubba Warner, who was as fat and as slow now as he was in the second grade, a grade he repeated three times before he learned to read. On this summer day, Estes and Bubba were on their way to the lake to participate in the annual fishing tournament that Estes was determined to win. For years he and Bubba had come close to winning, but always fell a pound or two short. This year, Estes was so determined that he had invested over four hundred dollars in fishing equipment—the best rods and reels, a sonar device to scout schools of fish, and his trusty shotgun, just in case he found a school close to the top that might be stunned into floating to the surface.

At the bait shop, Estes bragged about his expensive equipment as he opened pint after pint of worms, spilling the rich brown peat out on the counter and examining each batch for the roundest, plumpest worms while Bubba bought a case of beer and a bag of ice. They loaded the small fishing boat and set out to win the contest, and Estes vowed that with each catch he would drink a beer. But when noon approached, a still-sober Estes changed the rules and began drinking every time he baited his hook. Bubba was doing no better. Estes watched as Bubba threaded the worm on the barb of the hook.

"What the hell are you doing, Bubba?"

"Spitting on him for good luck. My granddaddy used to do it, and he caught fish by the truckload."

"That old man couldn't fish worth a damn."

"Well, we got to try something. All your fancy equipment hasn't had them jumping in the boat."

The two men quit talking and finished off the beer as shadows began to hover over the water in the cove. Bubba piloted the boat along the shoreline as Estes made one last attempt to land a bass to add to the day's measly catch. Failing once again, he took the ice chest filled with the day's catch—six or seven small bream—and pitched the whole thing into the lake.

"Let's get home, Bubba, and get us some beer."

Bubba maneuvered the boat through a thicket of weeds, trying to dock as close to the truck and trailer as possible. A bright streak of sunlight cut through the trees and reflected on the water, temporarily blinding Bubba, who almost ran the boat ashore.

"Damn you, Bubba."

Recovering his sight, Bubba navigated the boat back toward the open water, passing through the shallow, shaded water beneath an overhanging tree. As the boat moved into sunlight again, both Bubba and Estes saw that they were no longer alone in the boat. A fat water moccasin had dropped from a branch of the shade tree, and now lay on the floor of the boat. Before Bubba had a chance to reason with him, Estes had pulled his gun and killed the snake and the boat at the same time.

"I got him," Estes said as he stood in the bow of the boat, holding the tail end of a snake that hung down to a bloody headless end just above his knee. "That'll teach him."

"You could have killed me, Estes. What if we'd been in the middle of the lake instead of the cove?"

"You wouldn't have run into a damn tree in the middle of the lake, Bubba," Estes said, as he pitched the remains of the snake toward Bubba whose sudden shift in position sent Estes into the water. Estes grabbed the boat and pulled it the few feet to shore while Bubba sat in the stern with water up to his knees and his arms folded in front of him like a tribal chieftain.

"Get out of the boat."

Bubba obeyed and helped to pull the damaged vessel onto a secure spot of bank. Neither spoke as they climbed to the road to find the pickup. They soon spotted it, and as they came within spitting distance of the boat trailer, Estes noticed a boy fishing from the bank a few feet away. As he watched, the boy pulled in another fish which he unhooked and added to a thin rope stringer laden with fish. Again, he baited the hook, dropped it in the water, and as soon as it hit, pulled in another fish.

"Will you look at that," Estes said as he headed toward the boy. Estes cast a large shadow that engulfed the boy. Bubba, following behind, lost his footing and almost slid into the water. The boy was startled by the two large men smelling of beer. He stepped back out of the shadows and the sunset hit his skin which was the color of a roasted chestnut and seemed to radiate heat.

"How long you been fishing, boy?" Estes asked.

"Just a little while, sir."

"Did someone give you those fish?"

"No, sir, I caught them."

"Look, Estes." Bubba said. "All he's got is a cane with a little line on it and an old piece of cork from a wine bottle. You got a ton of equipment and only got six all day, but this kid's got a full stringer. So much for modern technology." Bubba grew silent as Estes glared at him.

"Get up, Bubba! What you got for bait, boy?" Estes continued asking questions.

"Found these worms," the boy said, pointing to a can that still had the bright green label. "The fish love 'em, but they sure do sting."

Estes picked up the can and then grabbed the boy with his free hand.

"You're coming with us," he said as the boy tried to pull away. "Come on. I won't hurt you." He handed the can to Bubba and with both hands lifted the child up off the ground and headed up the bank.

"I didn't do nothing," the boy protested as Estes called for Bubba who kept looking into the can. Finally, he pitched it away, and scrambled up the bank.

"Shit, Estes, they're moccasins."

Bubba jammed his heavy body behind the steering wheel as Estes calmed the boy. The pickup bounced up the dirt road as the boat trailer thrashed behind. Hitting the county road, they drove past Equality, which no longer had a doctor since Doc Campbell died, and set their sights on the hospital in Alex City. Before Bubba turned on the headlights, Estes looked at the venom-swollen hands that the boy held out like an aging arthritic.

Bubba hadn't stopped the truck before Estes had the boy in

the emergency room. Setting the bare black feet on the white floor, Estes began a slightly drunken monologue for the stately woman behind the admitting desk, who pushed her chair back against the wall to avoid Estes's breath as she tried several times to interrupt. Finally, a man in a white lab coat arrived, and Estes, grabbing the lapels, began to repeat the story.

"We don't admit coloreds." The man in the white coat had said the words several times before Estes heard them and fell silent. He looked out the door at the boy whose head was nodding and whose hands now hung at his sides like the udders of cows who had gone too long without milking.

"There's a clinic across town. Down Main across the tracks, three roads, then left." The man in the white coat held the door for Bubba and Estes as they loaded the boy into the pickup, then turned as it closed behind him.

Bubba drove down Main Street, running two red lights and crossing the train tracks with such force that the boat trailer was ripped off and rolled over in a ditch. Bubba was busy watching the trailer in the rearview mirror when he felt the boy kick his side. He looked at Estes and then at the boy whose body convulsed and with a final heave, went limp. Bubba ran the car off the road before regaining control and stopped abruptly on the shoulder as the red light of the state trooper car swirled in the side mirror.

"There's nothing to do now," the trooper said, looking in the window at a silent Estes cradling the body. "Why don't you throw it in the back and drop it off at the funeral home. We'll deal with it tomorrow."

"I want to take him home," Estes said without looking at the trooper.

"Where is home?"

"Couldn't be far from the cove."

"There's that old preacher that lives over by the bait shop. He might know him," Bubba said to the trooper, who called into the office and followed the pickup truck back to the cove. The trooper spoke with the preacher. Estes watched as they walked to the truck where the trooper shone a flashlight onto the face of the boy lying in his arms. Bubba stayed close behind the trooper and the preacher as he followed the patrol car down the narrow dirt road. The pickup lights illuminated the single-room structure while the preacher went inside.

Estes watched as the screen door opened slightly and child after child slipped out of the house. Finally, the preacher came out escorting a young woman still in her nightshirt. She raised her hand to shade her eyes from the bright headlights, and as she came closer, Estes opened the door and stepped out of the truck with the boy in his arms. The trooper shined the light at the boy's face, but the preacher pushed it away. She knew it was her son even in the darkness.

The preacher took the body and carried it toward the house as Estes told the story for the last time of the evening. "If only we'd gotten back sooner," he said over and over, as he stood before the boy's mother with his arms outstretched as if still holding her child. The mother's head was bowed. She never looked at Estes but watched instead the other children that had gathered about her feet. She reached out and shook Estes's hand and thanked him as she sent the curious children back toward the house. When the smallest child tripped and began to cry, the mother turned and lifted the baby to her hip, brushing off the dirt and gently kissing its forehead. She looked back at Estes.

"Did you bring the fish?"

Estes shook his head no. He was still shaking his head as the screen door closed behind her.

$\mathscr{I}$ am in the service of the queen . . . if this had been an actual emergency . . . she talks to angels . . . just a gigolo . . . knee-deep in the hoopla . . . 96 tears . . . in my white room with black curtains . . . a driving experience . . . desert island classics . . .

lola, l–o–l–a . . . wild thing . . . wild nights are . . . are you lonesome . . . are you . . . are you . . . they call her out . . .

Cordelia has been quiet for some time now. She listens to bits of radio and lies still, content with her surroundings. She is ready for the next chapter, the one nobody has ever written about. It's a new adventure and Cordelia always loved adventure. Children watch seven hours of television a day. They see murder and mayhem on a constant basis, but they almost never see anyone die a natural death. The entire structure of drama is based on conflict. An event takes place between two or more people, this event upsets the status quo, there is conflict leading to a denouement, and there is resolution. Everything is played out before three cameras, a shooting technique that originated with *I Love Lucy.*

There is an initial five-minute period to capture that attention of the viewer. Someone has to be shot, stabbed, or menaced— something must explode, crash or burn—no one is content with the stillness—no one appreciates the silence. But that is what so much of life is. The silences between the action. Cordelia is quiet and Mr. Delaney can't stand it. He wants her to sit up in bed and eat the food he brings, he wants her to tell him stories, he wants her to live, and in the enormous volume of his wants, he fails to hear Cordelia's silent explosion.

Where's Gabrielle?"

"She's on maternity leave. I'm Anthony, her replacement."

"Well, Gabrielle always looked after Cordelia."

"But she's on leave. I'm the new nurse."

"She was so still, I thought I should call somebody. I couldn't tell if . . ."

"She's still holding on. Still listening to those tunes, huh, Cordelia."

I'm goin' to Graceland . . .

"All right, Cordelia, but can't you find some Motown?"

"What was that."

"She's changing the stations, Mr. Delaney. She knows we're here. She just can't bring herself to chat with us, can you Cordelia? It's okay, though. I'll stop by every now and then."

"Aren't you going to take her to the hospital?"

"No. She has requested that no extreme measures be taken. She doesn't want to go to the hospital and we're not going to disturb her."

"What if she . . ."

"When Cordelia dies, Mr. Delaney, she will die on her own terms. That is the way she planned it and that is the way it's going to be. It was her choice."

"Well, I think some of the ladies from the church would want to be here."

"Whatever. Cordelia, I'll keep looking in on you."

"And I'll call my wife. Cordelia, I'm going to call the ladies in the prayer circle. They'll stop in to sit with you. They've been praying every day for you to get better. I'll call the preacher, too."

They have been praying for the wrong thing.

Drives a van. Your preacher drives a van. God help us."

Joe had watched from the porch as Stephen's hulking body climbed out of an old blue VW van. Adelaide could still hear Joe's voice. Joe had never cared much for preachers, and he was especially leery of this one. Stephen was a young man built more like a linebacker than a man of God, with shaggy hair and a personality like carbonated soda.

Adelaide greeted Stephen as he stepped onto the porch. "Hello, Reverend."

"Looks kinda irreverent to me," said Joe as Adelaide blushed.

"Don't mind him, Reverend, he's been like that for most of the forty years we've been married. It's a bit aggravating, but never dangerous. Have a seat. I'll get us some lemonade."

"Make mine stronger!" Joe yelled as Adelaide disappeared into the house. "Didn't mean to offend you, Reverend. I guess now that you're here we'll be hearing a lot of those Jesus rock songs blasting from the church."

"I don't—"

"When I went to church you didn't need a hymnal. We all knew the songs. We knew the rituals, too. Now that we merged, converged, and united, who the hell knows anything anymore. I might as well be a Catholic."

"I know what you mean, Joe. It does my heart good to go look out over the congregation and see them singing without a hymnal. I love those old standards. May I?" Stephen reached for the guitar standing against the wall. Joe nodded as the young man lifted the fine walnut instrument and admired the inlaid mother-of-pearl on the frets as he tightened the strings. He cradled the guitar as a jeweler would lift cut glass.

Joe watched, thinking Stephen's large knotty hands were too big to produce sound from his guitar. A familiar melody flooded the porch as Stephen's voice, crisp and clean, rose like a choirboy's.

"The sun is slowly sinking.
The day is almost done."

"Jump in any time, Joe," Stephen said without missing a note, and by the second verse, Joe's voice, rough and scratchy, blended sweetly with the voice of the visitor.

"That was lovely," said Adelaide as she stood in the door holding the lemonade. "You couldn't have picked a better song. 'The Darkest Hour' is Joe's favorite."

"I'll put the organist on alert, Joe. Then any time I see you at church, I'll be sure we sing it."

"It'll take more than that, Reverend."

Stephen saw Joe on the street or in the hardware store, but he had never pressed him to go to church. They continued to talk about music, and Joe sometimes offered suggestions for the Sunday hymns. Joe had boasted for weeks about his skill as a domino player. "Do you ever play, Steve, old boy?" Joe asked.

"Once in a while, Joe. I'd like to take you on someday."

Finally Stephen joined Joe and some of his friends in a match. Adelaide was somewhat appalled by Joe's childish bragging over the game.

"I believe this will be another ten points. It's a close one, Reverend, but you can't beat me. I guess you'll have to draw another domino. Maybe you'll draw a good one. The five-six would block the game."

As she had served them coffee, Adelaide noticed Stephen's hand poised above one of the marble game pieces. With a quick glance she saw that Stephen had the winning domino. She couldn't remember a time in the last year when Joe had lost.

While in the kitchen, she heard Joe's loud laughter and Stephen's voice, "You did it, Joe. I was sure I had you."

The reverend brought his cup into the kitchen as Adelaide stood on her tiptoes to return a pan to the shelf. "You threw the game, Reverend," she said as she strained to reach the shelf. Stephen took the pan and, without extending his arm fully, set it on the high shelf.

"What an awful thing to say, Adelaide. Besides, there'll be other games." And there were.

Adelaide, glancing at the living room, saw the table where Joe had fought hard over many games of dominoes. Sitting at that table, Joe had first challenged the new preacher to a game. She looked over her shoulder at Joe, but he did not respond. He'd not responded for over a year now, since he had suffered the stroke. He just stayed drawn up in a ball, like a baby. Adelaide didn't expect him to answer, but every now and then she was sure that Joe would reach up, rub her shoulders, and tell her that it had all been a dream. She patted the motionless body in the bed. "I have to go fix supper now, if you need anything . . ." Her voice trailed.

She moved aimlessly about the kitchen, which had once been her center of activity. The warm place where she could once close her eyes and find even the most obscure utensil or spice was now foreign. Even the location of a can opener was a mystery. She opened a can that she randomly selected from the cupboard and emptied it into a saucepan. For a brief moment she thought that she heard the strings of Joe's guitar. She stopped, and when the sound came again, she moved from the stove to the door of the kitchen.

Long ago she had positioned the sickroom dresser so that she could see Joe from the kitchen door. She hurried to look. Perhaps Joe would be sitting on the edge of the bed playing his guitar; perhaps it would be like one of those stories that leapt at her from the supermarket tabloids. She was afraid to look. She wanted so badly to believe. Joe lay as he had, motionless and fetal, and the sound of the guitar was just another trick of her exhaustion.

As she ate her soup, she remembered a time that had been easier for her. After Joe's stroke, there had been a continuous stream of people offering help. They stayed and brought food. But as time went on, fewer people came, choosing to help with new illnesses and dramatic deaths. When it became obvious that he was going to linger, they did not.

Adelaide thought of the first time she saw Joe as she smoothed the sheet on the bed. He was standing on a ladder painting this very house. You were so tall, I thought you didn't need that ladder. Later on toward evening, you brought me a leaf dotted with paint. Do you remember? Adelaide fluffed the pillows as she sat on the edge of the bed. You said the paint looked like a heart. It was an omen, you said. She began to rearrange the medicine bottles on the bedside table. It doesn't seem like forty-five years.

The evening dragged on into another day, as Adelaide carefully turned Joe's body to keep his lungs clear. She turned him every two hours which made sleep a useless exercise. The grandfather clock struck twelve. Midnight was her favorite time of the night because the chimes lasted the longest, filling the house with a temporary feeling of warmth. By one o'clock she felt the most alone and deserted. She hated the darkness and the quiet. She hated fighting her tired body and hearing the clock strike one single time, knowing that she had another entire day to be alone with her thoughts. There had been many of these mornings.

Joe had been the real beginning of her life. They had gone through so much together, suffered the Depression, seen boys from Equality that they had known since birth die in wars, seen assassinations and unrest. Equality was no longer the place of their youth. The South had changed and so had the world, but Joe had always made her feel safe. Now she felt as if they had spent their whole lives setting up dominoes end to end. Somewhere along the way, an unknown hand had pushed the first domino over, and they all began to fall, one after another, as their clicking together and tumbling grew louder and more intense until the sound disappeared. Adelaide wondered whether the silence came because all of the dominoes had fallen or whether they continued to fall and the quiet was merely deafness.

Several hours passed. Adelaide was so used to creating sounds in her mind that she didn't answer the knock at the door. When the sound continued, she looked out the curtain, saw the darkness still outside and wondered who would be calling at this hour. Stephen stood on the porch wearing jeans and a flannel shirt over a T-shirt. Even at this hour, as Adelaide opened the door and he stepped into the living room, his voice was clear and crisp.

"Couldn't sleep, Adelaide. God sent me out driving and I saw your light. . . ."

Before he could finish, Adelaide interrupted. She clenched her fingers, then turned and planted both fists into his chest as though he had been the one who had pushed the first domino. "There is no God. Look at Joe. I pray and pray." Adelaide turned away, shocked at her own outburst.

"What do you pray, Adelaide?"

"I pray that we make it through another day. I pray for each day." She caught her breath.

"And God answers your prayer, Adelaide."

Adelaide's head fell forward. She could no longer contain her emotion, and she wept aloud. Stephen wrapped her in his comforting hold as though he were her older brother instead of a man forty years her junior. A long time had passed since anyone had touched her. Her muscles tightened, only to relax as the reverend rocked her body back and forth.

"Now, why don't you make us some tea. Then you can go to bed. I'll stay here today," he said, and he walked with her to the kitchen.

Adelaide filled the kettle with water, putting it on the stove to boil. She entered the dining room to get some cups. Stephen's worn brown deck shoes sat empty by his chair. Adelaide looked at them. "Now I know why they call them 'boat' shoes," she said to no one. She placed the cups on a tray and stood by the kettle. The heat from the stove warmed her face.

"The sun is slowly sinking . . ."

She heard the opening line of Joe's favorite hymn. Stephen's voice was unmistakable, filling the house and making it seem alive. Everything seemed back to normal with her puttering in the kitchen, the reverend singing, and Joe. Now was the time for Joe to come in, this was his cue. She would hold her breath for one last time and wait for him to . . .

"The narrow way leads home . . ."

No Joe. She moved to the door and looked at Joe's reflection in the mirror. He was not alone. Beside his emaciated body lay the reverend who cradled Joe's head while continuing to sing. Even though the reverend was enormous in the bed, and even though he wore jeans, and his big toe stuck through his socks, Adelaide thought of a mother and child as the kettle whistled.

"Lay down your soul at Jesus' feet . . ."

Adelaide poured the boiling water into the teapot and set it on the tray. Joe would never sing again. He would never play the guitar or dominoes, nor would he ever warm her feet in the bed. Lifting the tray and walking toward the dining room, she paused at the door to take a last look in the mirror.

"The darkest hour is just before dawn."

As Adelaide watched, Joe's body relaxed for the first time in a year. She had forgotten how tall Joe was. She saw the reverend straightening the body under the folds of the quilt, and for a second the reflection became a pietà. The cups on the tray rattled, and Adelaide moved to the table. The ordeal was over.

Stephen could have stopped singing, but he didn't. He sang all the verses, growing louder with each chorus. At the final chorus, Adelaide looked into the sickroom. Joe's body now lay straight in the center of the bed as the reverend carefully smoothed the bedding over him, making sure there were no wrinkles in the quilt.

Stephen joined her at the table, pausing briefly to slip into his shoes. Sitting in the chair beside Adelaide, he touched her hand.

"How about my tea?" he said, and Adelaide looked up and squeezed his hand momentarily before pouring the tea.

"What do you take in your tea?"

"A tad of milk."

Adelaide poured three drops of cold white milk into the cup, watching as they hit the amber liquid and began to diffuse. She made tiny waves with the spoon, unaware that the sun had risen.

*D*eath doesn't make a good movie. Violence makes the movie, but death, the actual death, unless inflicted in a violent manner, holds little appeal. Cordelia has turned off the radio. This is the only denouement the story will have. Any conflict that may have occurred has been reconciled.

The first movie they ever showed in Equality was *Gone With the Wind*. The theater opened seven years after the premier in Atlanta. Every time a new theater opened in the South, they brought back Rhett and Scarlet. It was a way to hold on to the memory. Now there are no new theaters in the South, *Gone With the Wind* has been shrunk for the nineteen-inch screen and packaged in video boxes. Atlanta burns like a fireplace.

Now, Cordelia sees only the small movies in her mind. There is no theater in Equality; it closed in the 1960s. The last movie flickers just behind her eyes as faint and as far away as the last movie they showed in Equality.

*I*t was Saturday night in Equality. In Jake's Pharmacy, several girls from the high school had gathered around the card rack reading birthday greetings to each other as the scent of Evening in Paris cologne mixed with Russell Stover chocolates. The girls might have been at the picture show this Saturday if the movie had not been *Bombshell,* starring Jean Harlow. Though it had been five years since the movie came out and over a year since Jean Harlow had died, the reputation of the movie and the star preceded the showing. No self-respecting woman in Equality would be caught in the company of Jean Harlow, even if she was just a projection on the screen.

"I know how she died," Rose said to the girls as she fanned herself with a card. Rose Wiley was their natural leader by default. Even at her tender age, most people approached her in the same manner you approached a skunk. If you saw it, you would turn and depart, but if it saw you, well, you would try not to make it mad or it might cause a stink. The other young women seemed disinterested in Rose's general statement, but Lenora looked up from her card.

"Who?" she asked.

"Jean Harlow."

The statement intrigued Lenora, who was fascinated with Jean Harlow. Several times during the past week she had wandered by the picture show box office to look at the stills from the movie. The fact that Harlow died at a young age caused her to be a mystery. Lenora was anxious to learn more, and since Rose was the only girl their age who was privy to regular copies of *Photoplay,* she was convinced that if anyone in Equality knew the exact facts of Jean Harlow's death it would be Rose.

"It was her appendix," Rose said, stretching out the words like day-old taffy.

The girls were less than enthusiastic over such a simple ailment, moving on to the get-well card section. Lenora began to tell a story about her brother's appendectomy when Rose intervened to explain the euphemism.

"Don't you understand?" she asked. "It was not like your brother's, silly. Regaining the attention of the group, she continued.

"Do you remember Blanche, that colored woman that cooked for us for a while? Well, Blanche had a daughter who got into trouble, and Blanche sent her away to Chicago for the operation and then she could never have children."

"What kind of trouble?" Lenora asked.

Rose seemed astounded at Lenora's lack of knowledge on such important matters.

"She was going to have a baby. Then, after Chicago, no baby. Got it, Lenora? Well, the same thing happened to Jean Harlow, only the operation failed, and she died."

As Rose was explaining this, the gathering became distracted as Jennings Potter came into view. Jennings had just moved to Equality. His mother had grown up there but had left town with a jazz musician whom she met in Mobile. They had roamed all over the country until the drummer died, and now Jennings and his mother had come home to live. Lenora had a crush on Jennings, and she had not been good about hiding her feelings for him. For her, he represented everything that she wasn't and would never be. He was tall and handsome. He had traveled all over the country, affording him a worldly outlook beyond his years. Lenora knew that he wouldn't be interested in a girl who had been born in the country and didn't even know how Jean Harlow died.

When Rose saw that Jennings was in earshot, she played with Lenora like a June bug on a string.

"Hello, Jennings," Rose said.

"Hello, ladies." The girls nodded and giggled nervously, but Rose, looking back and forth between Lenora and Jennings, continued to speak.

"Jennings, we were just talking about Jean Harlow and how she died. It was terrible, wasn't it? You know what I heard? You tell him, Lenora. Tell him how she died." Lenora was speechless, her face turning the color of a ripened tomato.

"I'll tell you, Jennings," Rose's voice rose in delight. "It was an appendix, the poor thing."

The girls were startled by Rose's forward attitude with

Jennings. Few of them had ever even whispered about such things, much less broached the subject in a public place with a young man present. The girls began to fall silently away like petals.

"Abscessed tooth," Jennings said as the interest of the crowd picked up.

"What?"

"Jean Harlow. Her tooth abscessed. It wouldn't normally kill you, but her mother belonged to this religious group that doesn't believe in doctors. She got blood poisoning, and she died. It's a shame. She was a good actress."

The girls listened intently, forming a cluster behind Rose. Jennings cast his eyes toward Lenora. He had watched her from the pharmacy window and had come inside to see if he might buy her a Coca-Cola. He had not been in Equality long enough to be warned about Rose.

"Where did you get that story?" Rose asked.

"My dad knew someone who knew the family," Jennings said.

"California, that's where your father died, wasn't it? Dental problems?"

"Car wreck. I identified the body." Jennings looked directly at Rose. He had left her no way out but to attack him, and smiling a half-smile more out of pity than anything else, he retreated rather than confront Rose any more.

"Lenora, can I walk you home?" Jennings asked.

Lenora was shocked by this request but would have done almost anything to get away from Rose. Outside she apologized for her friend and for his father's death as though the only words in her vocabulary were "I'm sorry." Fighting to change the subject, she asked him about the famous people he had met in California.

"Did you ever meet her?"

"Jean Harlow? Never."

"Did you really identify the body?"

"Someone had to. My mother was hurt."

"I couldn't do it. I mean looking at a dead person. I just couldn't do it. I've never seen anybody who was dead. I did see my grandfather's coffin, but not him. Not after he was dead. I've never even been to a funeral. I stayed with the lady next door when Grandpa was buried. I wanted to go. I wanted to see him but they wouldn't let me. I don't know why, but after that, well, I just never had the opportunity, I guess. I wish I had seen him so I would have known, or at least seen one." Lenora had thought to herself several sentences before that she should stop talking, but her nervousness took over, and now she stood silently, having run out of things to say. Jennings, putting his arm around her shoulder, broke the silence.

"It's not a hard wish. I mean, do you really want to see a body?"

Lenora nodded. It would certainly be different, and besides, there was little else to do in Equality on a Saturday night. Jennings took her arm, leading her across the street, changing their direction.

"Sometimes they won't let children go to funerals, and then they feel excluded. The body is the same, but the spirit is gone." Jennings's voice was calm yet gentle as he led Lenora up the street, crossing the bridge over the train tracks and up a slight incline that had once been the expansive front yard of a boarding house. Lenora remembered when the house stood on the lot shaded by a magnolia tree whose branches hung almost to the ground, but whose roots now lay under the gravel parking lot of Reed's Funeral Home. As Lenora stood poised at the door ready to enter, Jennings laid out all the details.

"It's Anna Stanley. She was eleven. The youngest Stanley girl. Rheumatic fever."

Inside there was a bright foyer that bore a striking resemblance to the living room in the Methodist parsonage, with couches and chairs and a coffee table with tiny claw feet. There were notices for three chapels on the wall over an oak credenza. All but one were blank. The Chapel C board displayed the answers to the basic questions that anyone would need to know. Name. Anna Lee Stanley. Church. Shiloh Baptist. Day. Tuesday. Time. Eleven o'clock. Even with all this information, Lenora had a hard time picturing Anna in her mind, though she knew she had seen her many times.

Jennings led her down a narrow hallway past Chapels A and B. Outside of Chapel C, they paused at a round table covered with a navy velvet cloth. On it lay the visitors' book that each signed, Lenora in bold sweeping print as though to make up for the absence of the name in her grandfather's book.

Inside the room, they were met by a man in a black wool suit that smelled of cedar. Jennings shook his hand and expressed his regrets, recalling his own father's death just a year before. Lenora merely nodded and cast her eyes toward the worn beige carpet. For the first time, as she and Jennings moved closer to the casket, Lenora began to regret the trip to the funeral home.

The casket lay before them like an opened jewelry box whose music had been silenced. The stark white enamel reflected even the dim lamp in the chapel. The pink satin interior, crisply smocked, matched the spray of pink roses that rested prostrate on the lower half of the box. Lenora raised her eyes and looked at the body. For a moment she thought that it was not real. The child was perfectly still, like a Christmas doll newly unwrapped. Nothing about Anna's appearance gave signs of sickness or death. She wore a white dotted Swiss dress whose pale pink dots stood on the fabric like the chill bumps that stood on Lenora's arms. A dusty pink bow circled the child's waist as the flared skirt disappeared under the closed half-top of the casket. Her skin was porcelain down to its cool touch, and ringlets of blonde hair framed a face in repose with closed eyes. They stood there only a minute before walking out, and they had crossed the bridge before either spoke.

Thanks, Jennings."

He held Lenora's hand tightly as he walked her home, passing the hardware store, the pharmacy, and the picture-show box office which sat empty in the darkness.

$\mathcal{H}$ow does it end? There is no answer to that question. An omniscient narrator is only omniscient as long there is a storyteller. God created man in his own image or vice versa. Without Cordelia, I cease to be omniscient. In a short time, I will crash to the ground, saved by Cordelia's rising up to catch me as I fall, uniting us in a silent flight. My falling will become her art. Michelangelo believed that the greatest artist had no conception which single block of marble did not potentially contain within its mass an image. But he knew that only a hand obedient to the mind could penetrate the marble and discover that image. With each chunk of marble, Michelangelo believed that a figure resided within and his job was to liberate that form from the cold confines of the stone.

Andrei Tarkovsky believed that for a director, the job was to sculpt time. He would state that just as a sculptor takes a lump of marble, and inwardly conscious of the features of his finished piece, removes everything that is not part of it—so the filmmaker, from a lump of time made up of enormous, solid clusters of living facts, cuts off and discards whatever he does not need.

A life is an assemblage. From the time you're born, you begin to pull bits and pieces toward you, keeping some, discarding others, arranging pebbles, feathers, Vivaldi's "Cello Concerto in G," memories, stories from childhood, Dior earrings, Granddad's pocketknife, an Elvis lighter, books, movies, packets of letters tied with ribbon, all in a large colorful tin filled by a hand obedient to the mind.

When it ends for Cordelia, it will end for both of us and I won't be able to tell you, for I will no longer have a voice. There will be no explosions or fires, no wailing or keening, no sound at all. Just a final sigh, a last breath in the stillness. That will be the end as I know it. What she feels, what the other side looks like, if there is another side, is the one book that has never been written.

There is so much that I do not know and so much I will never be able to tell you. How will it end? I don't know, but there are some things I am sure of.

That there is no black or white, only infinite shades of gray.

That Constantinople is now Istanbul and neither is the capital of Turkey.

That Adam Duritz wants to be Bob Dylan, but Mr. Jones wants to be someone a bit more funky.

That the pain of Saint Anthony's Fire can only be eased by dancing.

And if there is a Heaven, Janis Joplin will be waiting, and chalcedony grows after the sun has set and the air is still warm, and the best watch to own is a broken watch, and the cello is the most feminine of all musical instruments, and the last line of *Gone With the Wind* is "Tomorrow is another day," and the capital of Somalia is Mogadishu.

Cordelia's Final Reading List

Kathy Acker, *Blood and Guts in High School*
Diane Apostolos-Cappadona, *Dictionary of Christian Art*
Tadeusz Borowski, *This Way for the Gas, Ladies and Gentlemen*
Paul Bowles, *The Sheltering Sky*
Kate Braverman, *Dropping In*
Olga Broumas, *Perpetua*
Truman Capote, *Other Voices, Other Rooms*
Paul Celan, *The Last Poems of Paul Celan*
Roald Dahl, *The Complete Stories of Roahl Dahl*
Louise DeSalvo and Mitchell Leaska, eds. *The Letters of Vita Sackville-West to Virginia Woolf.*
William Faulkner, *The Sound and the Fury*
F. Scott Fitzgerald, *The Great Gatsby*
Margaret Rose Gladney, ed., *How Am I to Be Heard: The Letters of Lillian Smith*
Martha Graham, *Blood Memory*
Amy Hempel, *Reason to Live*
Wayne Koestenbaum, *The Queen's Throat*
Julia Kristeva, *Proust and the Sense of Time*
Mitchell Leaska and John Phillips, eds., *Violet to Vita: The Letters of Violet Trefusis to Vita Sackville-West*
Harper Lee, *To Kill a Mockingbird*
Primo Levi, *The Drowned and the Saved*
Malcolm Lowry, *Under the Volcano*
Carole Maso, *Ava*

Christiane Meyer-Thoss, *Louise Bourgeois: Designing for Free Fall*
Margaret Mitchell, *Gone With the Wind*
Vladimir Nabokov, *Lolita*
Nigel Nicolson and Joanne Trautman, eds. *The Letters of Virginia Woolf*
Lorine Niedecker, *From the Far Condensery*
Breece D'J Pancake, *The Stories of Breece D'J Pancake*
Sylvia Plath, *The Bell Jar*
Ned Rorem, *Knowing When to Stop*
Alina Reyes, *The Butcher*
John Kennedy Toole, *A Confederacy of Dunces*
Hildegard von Bingen, *Symphonia*
Andrei Tarkovsky, *Sculpting in Time*
Hugo Vickers, *Loving Garbo*
Walt Whitman, *A Song of Myself*
Jeanette Winterson, *The Passion*